P9-CQQ-012

NINE MUST DIE

Center Point
Large Print

Also by Lee E. Wells and available from Center Point Large Print:

The Naked Land
Tarnished Star
Treachery Pass
Vulture's Gold
The Devil's Range

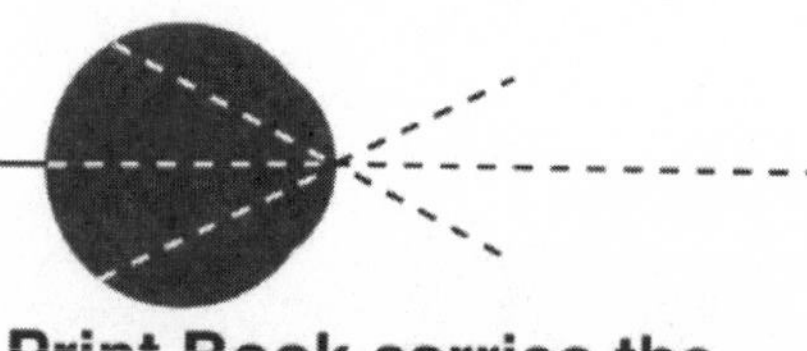

NINE MUST DIE

LEE E. WELLS

CENTER POINT LARGE PRINT
THORNDIKE, MAINE

This Center Point Large Print edition
is published in the year 2018 by arrangement with
Golden West Literary Agency.

First US edition: Berkley

The text of this Large Print edition is unabridged.
In other aspects, this book may vary
from the original edition.
Printed in the United States of America
on permanent paper.
Set in 16-point Times New Roman type.

ISBN: 978-1-64358-033-3 (hardcover)
ISBN: 978-1-64358-037-1 (paperback)

Library of Congress Cataloging-in-Publication Data

Names: Wells, Lee E., 1907-1982, author.
Title: Nine must die / Lee E. Wells.
Description: Center Point Large Print edition. | Thorndike, Maine :
Center Point Large Print, 2018.
Identifiers: LCCN 2018042056| ISBN 9781643580333
(hardcover : alk. paper) | ISBN 9781643580371
(paperback : alk. paper)
Subjects: LCSH: War stories. | Western stories. | Vendetta—Fiction. |
Outlaws—Fiction. | Large type books.
Classification: LCC PS3545.E5425 N56 2018 | DDC 813/.54—dc23
LC record available at https://lccn.loc.gov/2018042056

NINE MUST DIE

1

It was quiet, unnaturally so, and the setting sun sent long distorted shadows easterly of the wagon. Each leaf hung motionless and clearly defined. The man who had taken the bullet lay sprawled just outside the wall of bushes and trees where his companions lurked.

Over two hours ago, his right leg had slowly straightened and since then he had remained motionless, bald head catching a dull reflection of the sun, his fingers taloned in the dirt. His gun would be over to the right somewhere, hidden in the grass.

The two horses, still in the traces, stood hip-shot, heads drooping. Fortunately, they were fed and watered at the nooning. Just as fortunately, Wayne Nelson had told his wife it was too hot to push hard. They had remained in the black shadow of the wagon, where Wayne spread blankets and brought the chests of dishes and supplies.

They had given Abbie some protection when the outlaws struck. Wayne had checked the horses and started back along the wagon to load up when a bullet whipped before his face and thudded info the wagon bed. He made a long dive to the wagon, a swift roll under it as Abbie's rifle cracked just above him.

There were graphic slivers of impressions—horsemen charging and bullets shrieking a high protest off the broad, iron wheel rims; his heavy Colt bucking in his hand; a detached, impersonal wonder that Abbie did not show panic as her calm shooting brought the leading horseman tumbling from his saddle.

Then Wayne had dropped the man who lay in full sight and the first attack had broken, the horsemen fading back into the bushes. Wayne frantically manhandled the chests into a barricade. There was a second attack soon after. The outlaws came afoot, using bushes and high grass to conceal their encircling movement. Wayne's Colt and Abbie's rifle beat that off, and there were at least two more wounded back in the greenery.

Now, the silence had a false tranquility. The killers were there, waiting. At first, two horses, a heavy wagon loaded with furniture, gewgaws, maybe jewelry and money, had attracted the outlaws. But a man and woman had beaten off two attacks, killed one or more, wounded as many. Renegade pride couldn't let them get away.

Wayne licked his dry lips and considered the lengthening shadows. The sun dropped westward with alarming speed. Abbie stirred and his eyes cut to her. Her face was as fine-cut as a cameo. Little sweat beads stood on her high forehead just below the roots of her dark bronze hair and along her full upper lip, perhaps a little irregular for perfect beauty but tender and passionate, as Wayne knew.

Sea green eyes turned to him and her slender hand released the rifle long enough to brush a wisp of hair from the long, smooth plane of her cheek. Her voice was low and firm. "What will they do?"

His gray eyes grew bleak. "Wait until dark."

She turned that over in her mind. "We won't have much of a chance, will we?

"No moon . . . it'll be dark. They'll slip up on us. We might get a chance at one—or two, but . . .

"They'll get us," she concluded evenly.

Her eyes searched the tricky shadows and half-lights of the bushes and he caught a slight tremble of her chin, swiftly gone. He looked out from under the wagon, jaw setting until a muscle rippled under tanned skin and line slashed down from nose to the corners of his long, irregular mouth, thinned now.

"Abbie."

She looked around. His long body lay stretched out by the rear wheel and she noticed again the width of his shoulders and depth of his chest. His checked shirt sleeves were rolled up on his muscular arms, moistened with sweat. She knew the hard, possessive tenderness of those arms. She studied his face; the long, angular plane from cheekbone to firm jaw, the slight shadow of a cleft in the broad chin, the little crooked break in the high ridge of his nose. His gray eyes, holding hers with a strange, tortured expression, were in startling contrast to the raven black sweep of his brows and the equally black hair that clung tightly to his head in moist ringlets.

His strong teeth held his lower lip an instant. "Abbie, they won't kill you right off if they can help it. They'll want you—"

"They won't have me, Wayne. I promise you."

He looked at the Colt in his hand, the bright gleam of the steel. His voice lowered in a note of false hope. "If we can't beat them off, I'll—take care of it."

"I know, darling. Don't think of it."

He looked at the cascade of coppery hair down her slim back, the push of full breasts against her gingham dress, the suggested lines of her long, shapely legs. He looked hastily away.

"Four months married, and all the things we planned! We'd get out of Virginia and let the Yanks have what's left. We'd make a new world all our own. A hell of a thing, Abbie! The way it's going to end."

"Maybe . . ." She passed her hand over her eyes and her throat contracted. She blinked away the tears and, needing him, turned to crawl to his side.

Wayne saw a slight movement in a bush. He held the Colt poised a second. Abbie froze as his finger tightened and the Colt's roaring crash shattered the silence. There was a yell, the bushes threshed, and then silence.

"Hope I killed him," Wayne said fervently.

Both scanned the bushes. Nothing moved, and again the hot, oppressive silence settled on the swale. Then a shot rang out and the bullet whipped between the wagon bed and the low barricade. Wayne saw a wisp of smoke and placed shots above and below it. An angry, defiant yell answered him.

"They'll wait now. We got that long, Abbie."

"The rest of our lives," she said with a twisted smile and then could hold herself no longer. "Oh, Wayne! Darling!"

She scrambled to him and threw herself upon him, her wet cheeks against his. He kissed her hair, her lips, tasted salt of tears.

His head lifted spasmodically when a rebel yell keened from somewhere beyond the bushes. The silence shattered in a fusillade of shots and Wayne heard a rolling thunder of hoofs. Surprised and frightened yells sounded and a bush swayed frantically. Wayne's eyes widened in unbelieving hope and Abbie lay tense and motionless in his arms.

Two riders burst out of the trees, spurs ripping along their horses' flanks. They looked back, paying no attention to the wagon. Wayne thrust Abbie away, brought up his gun, but by then the men had disappeared. There was another burst of shots, a fading yell and the swale was empty.

A rider appeared, then a second. Abbie grabbed up her rifle, chin set. Wayne called sharply, "Wait, Abbie!"

The first rider held a rifle loosely in his right hand and, just behind him, the second man edged forward, holstering a revolver. Wayne dogged back the hammer of his gun and his eyes cut to the right when he heard sounds of other riders.

The first rider drew rein. "Halloo! the wagon! Are you all right?"

The weakness of relief swept over Wayne and his head dropped down on his forearm. His body felt as though the substance of his bones had melted. Then life surged back and he called an answer. He grabbed Abbie, kissed her fiercely, and swiftly crawled from under the wagon as half a dozen more riders came into the open.

Wayne hurried to the first rider, hand extended in welcome. "That rebel yell sounded sweet as Gabriel's trumpet, sir! My wife and me—well—we can't thank you, but—"

"Why, no thanks." The man leaned down to clasp his hand, then courteously swept off his broad-brimmed hat to Abbie. He had a gentle, deep-grooved face aged by experience, though the years showed in the iron gray of his hair. His voice, gentle as his face, was full and grave. "I'm Frank Burrud, at your service."

"You *have* served us, sir," Abbie said fervently. "I think we had until dark to live. What brought you?"

"Shooting," the second rider said. He was tall and rangy, perhaps five years younger than Wayne. When they turned to him, his cheeks flamed and his brown eyes moved away as he uncomfortably ran his knuckles along his bony jaw. He jerked off his hat, disclosing brown hair, thick and crudely cut at the back of his sunburned neck.

"This is Lew Kearney," Burrud said. He turned to the other six as they crowded close and introduced them.

They were a blur of faces and names, but Wayne and Abbie felt as though they faced veritable warriors of the Lord, sent in this miraculous fashion. The sheer ecstasy of knowing they would live made them babble and gave them a confused impression of mounted, armed men of varied sizes and ages. Only Frank Burrud and Lew Kearney stood out clearly for the moment, Wayne and Abbie could only make out one statement in all the confusion and talk. These men, as a group, were heading for New Mexico and might go as far as Arizona.

A glance at the sky, after they buried the baldheaded man and two others, told them there was little left to the day. Wayne asked them to share supper and Burrud, giving the others a swift, questioning glance, accepted with grave thanks. "Besides, your friends might be back."

By now, Wayne could sort impressions, associate names with faces. He noticed the precision with which the men worked, gathering wood and water, in taking over the preparation of the meal from Abbie, in the way they picketed their horses. Either they had traveled long and far as a group, or this was the deep-drilled habits of the army. He had known it himself for four years, ending a little over six months ago.

He mentioned it to Frank, who smiled. "Thought I saw it in you, too."

"First Virginia," Wayne answered the unspoken question. "From First Manassas to Appomattox."

These eight, like Wayne, had served under the Stars and Bars, in varying theaters of war, all knowing battle, even to Lew Kearney. Like Wayne, they had been cast adrift when the war ended.

Each, from what little was said, returned to what had been home. So had Wayne. He remembered the ravaged countryside and the great void that friends, dead on a dozen battlefields, made by an absence that would never end.

Wayne noticed that so long as the talk was general, it was easy and friendly. But there was subtle withdrawal or clear evasion if he inadvertently touched on personal matters. The conversation would die out for a moment, then one of them would mention a battle or a place in their journey westward and talk would start again.

Still, Wayne knew what must have happened, since he was also part of the pattern. Within a matter of a fortnight back home, he had seen the utter futility of trying to fit in. He decided to strike out into the Southwest where an ex-Johnny Reb would find acceptance. So with these men. Wayne wondered how, each coming from some far-off place, they had met and had become such a smooth-working unit.

In one way, Wayne was far luckier than any of them. He had Abbie. Now and then he caught the men covertly admiring her. It gave Wayne a feeling of pride and content. For four years of battle, march and more battle, before campfire or on lonely sentry duty, he had dreamed of the girl down the road.

She had also remembered the boy down the road. Within two months they were married. Wayne managed to trade and dicker for a team, wagon and the tools necessary to start a new life somewhere westerly.

He emerged from memories as the talk moved on. Abbie now and then looked toward the darkness beyond the reach of the fire. The outlaws were gone but from this day on she would be fearful of sudden attack. He studied Burrud, young Kearney, the others—eight well-armed men. Sometime tomorrow they would part and Wayne would tool his lone wagon westward.

He impulsively asked, “You’re going to New Mexico . . . Arizona?”

Frank nodded. “Lordsburg, Benson, Tucson—maybe as far north as Prescott, though that’s Yankee country. Depends on how things work out.”

“Look, all of us are going the same way. I know a team and loaded wagon would hold down mounted men, but I hope you’re not in that much of a hurry. . . .”

He sensed an immediate withdrawal. They looked at Frank, whose brow knitted. “I don’t know, Nelson.”

Wayne made a sweeping gesture toward the outer darkness. “Abbie and me, we’re just a lone wagon, ripe pickings for any outlaw band. It won’t be long before we’re in Apache country. Our luck nearly run out today except you came along. But we can’t always depend on something like that. A man can take a chance. Abbie’s something else.”

They sat very still. It was there again, that invisible wall. Abbie felt it. Her hand touched Wayne’s wrist. “We’d only hold these gentlemen back. We can’t add our problems to theirs.”

The wavering light of the fire deepened the grooves in Frank’s gentle face. “I . . . don’t know, Nelson. It’s something to think on. I—we’ll decide come morning.”

Soon after, as though by unspoken command, they turned to their blankets and the fire died down. Some time deep in the night, Wayne's eyes snapped open. He lay quite still, trying to place the small sound that had awakened him. His hand eased down under the blanket to the holstered gun at his side as his eyes cut to Abbie's still form, then to the faint sparks of the near-dead fire.

The sound came again. Off in the darkness, men talked in low voices. The eight men had left the fire, their blankets tossed aside. The voices lifted, then died again.

Wayne leaned on one elbow. He tried unsuccessfully to pierce the outer darkness. The voices continued, first one and then another. Wayne sank back on his blankets. For a time he lay looking up at the night sky and then he heard the men return, walking softly and easing into their blankets.

They were up before dawn and there was no sign of the nocturnal conference as the men built up the fire, cut wood, brought water. But after breakfast as Wayne repacked the wagon, Frank Burrud came over. "This country is mean for a lone wagon—and it'll get worse further on. We'd enjoy to have your company for a spell."

Wayne's surprised elation was checked by memory of the argument. "I don't want to be a burden, and neither would Abbie. If you're in a hurry—"

"Hush, now! You're purely welcome and there's no more to be said." Frank chuckled. "Was it just you, ugly as you are, it might be different. But for Mrs. Nelson's sake, we'll manage to put up with you."

Wayne laughed and they shook hands.

The eight men, their decision made, fully accepted Wayne and Abbie. They made a smooth-working group. Nine well-armed, alert men discouraged outlaws or Indians and the days passed with no more than the normal incidents of the trail.

More important, Wayne and Abbie came to know the eight and each day increased their liking, but with a slight reservation about Bedford Drumbo. Bed was short, false fat accented by his round, full face with black, shaggy brows. He was the strongest of the group, a blacksmith and ironmonger.

He was quick to help but he had an innate coarseness. He was all courtesy but his speech had an elusive double meaning. His black eyes would follow Abbie as she moved about the fire as though he looked right through her dress.

Scipio Adams, lean and cadaverous, investigated Wayne's tool chest and the wagon interior began to change. Careful joining and shrewd use of small space created snug cabinets and lockers that delighted Abbie. Skip responded to her thanks with a death's head grin and a deep, awkward flush on his sallow cheeks.

Each night, after the meal, Joel Ramsey brought his guitar and, moon-face alight, struck a few chords and sang familiar melodies in an untrained Irish tenor. Even in butternut trousers stuffed into scarred boots, a cartridge-studded belt around his waist, Joel looked the barkeeper he had been. He had China blue eyes, rounded cheeks, straight brown hair that he kept neatly combed, always one lock curling down over his forehead.

Just beyond the Pecos, they came on a scabrous collection of adobe houses. They camped just west of the village to make minor repairs on the wagon and Wayne wandered into the town's single cantina. He never forgot how Hal Grayson and Vic Hayes suddenly appeared when three swart men figured Wayne could be safely worked into a gunfight. The two blond giants changed things in a hurry.

Jesse Burrud had Frank's gentle face and deep voice. His hair was not quite as gray but he had the same slow patience of his elder brother, the mark of men who till the soil. Heavy, rough hands had the surprising touch of the innate healer and he had the instinctive knowledge of the source of an illness and the homespun remedy for it, as

Abbie discovered when she was suddenly taken with a brief, high fever.

So they pushed beyond El Paso and across New Mexico into Arizona, through Apacheria. They swung south to avoid Cochise' stronghold and worked their way to Tucson. Though they came on the blackened monuments of Apache raids and twice saw signal fires on distant peaks, they somehow escaped the attention of these fierce desert marauders.

By now it seemed to Wayne they had traveled together since the beginning of time and he also *knew* the eight were bound together by some mystery in their past. Though each of them counted him and Abbie as friends, yet there was some shadowy area they guarded. It was a subtle watchfulness just below the surface of the normal, easy routine of the days.

Abbie mentioned it. Once she wondered, disbelieving herself, if they might not have been outlaws back in their homes. Wayne was sure they were not. They fled hard times, as he and Abbie did . . . but there was something more.

It was a relief to enter Tucson, a fascination in wandering streets where old adobe and new frame channeled the bustle of American business and the slow, easy way of the *mañana* people. Yet it disappointed them. Wayne planned to look about for a farm. He soon found he had a strange reluctance to tie himself down to this place. It "felt" strange and wrong. He heard talk of the new towns to the north, springing up along the rivers, near the mines, along the established stage and freighting roads. The real promise of the new land lay there. He spoke to Abbie. She was confused by this Arizona country, wearied by the long trip and she could only helplessly shake her head.

That night, Lew Kearney came to the wagon. The eight camped but a short distance away and often one or more of them would visit. Lew took supper with them and, over a cup of coffee, said that the eight would be riding north within a day or two. "There's a town up there on the banks of the Gila. They call it Florence. From what we hear, it sort of fits us."

"Why?" Wayne asked.

"There's good land along the river. Frank and Jesse plan to farm. There's mines to the north where some of us could get work. They say the town'll grow fast. So, we've decided to go." He looked deep into the fire and a shadow passed over his face. "Besides, it's small and out of the way. We like that."

Wayne sat thoughtfully while Lew slowly finished his coffee. Wayne looked at Abbie several times and said suddenly, "Well, now! That's it. We'll go with you."

Lew looked up, at first pleased and then uncertain. “I don’t know, Wayne—maybe better talk to ’em.”

Wayne arose, hitched at his belt. “I’ll do that—now. Give him more coffee, Abbie. I’ll be back directly.”

By now, Wayne knew them well enough to make a flat statement that he’d go with them and stood by while they argued it out. Drumbo and Grayson looked dubious and made a few minor objections without much heat. They sounded relieved when the Burrud brothers overruled them.

So, late one warm January afternoon, a dusty cavalcade pushed across a desert plain studded with saguaro toward a huddle of adobes and stores that marked Florence. Just beyond flowed the Gila. Northward beyond the river, a low line of hills stood painted against a washed sky, a road of sorts emerging from it.

The cavalcade moved slowly into the main street of the town. The wagon creaked, Wayne driving, Abbie sitting primly beside him, her green eyes alight with curiosity about this place that could be home. Eight trail-weary riders flanked the wagon.

Their entrance brought excitement. Women stood in doorways to watch them ride by. A dog came yapping out, missed losing its head by a scant inch to the kick of Grayson’s horse, and tore ky-yi-ing back to safety. A Papago Indian watched them in stolid silence.

They came to a small double line of stores and saloons. Wayne had planned to drive through the town and camp somewhere along the river bank this first night.

Canby Tryon, a pudgy little man with a fierce mustache and the jaw of a bulldog, stood at the window of his freighting office and shrewdly eyed the military bearing of the newcomers. He spoke over his shoulder to Lorain. "Looks like the town's growing. Might get a teamster or two out of that bunch."

With a rustle, Lorain arose from the desk and stepped to the door. She stood framed against the dark interior, a tall, fair girl whose golden hair captured some of the desert sun. Her blue eyes swept the group and held on the youngest.

At the same moment, Lew Kearney looked directly at her. Their eyes met, held, but in another moment the tall young man had ridden on. Lorain, not quite understanding the swift beat of her heart, felt that something important had happened. She returned to her desk, disturbed and wondering.

Further down the street, Ewing Vance yawned behind his bar. His saloon was empty for the moment. He circled the bar, pushed open the batwings and stepped out on the canopied porch.

The wagon and the outriders had just approached and Ewing's flecked green eyes lighted with pleasure. Newcomers, nine men—undoubtedly future patrons of his Gila Saloon. Suddenly his eyes became circles of horrified surprise. One of those men—one of those faces—had been seared into his memory.

With a strangled sound, he plunged back through the batwings. He strode toward the bar and the gun he kept there. He brought up short, lips working, but reason beginning to show again in his eyes.

He turned sharply, pushed open a door at the rear of the big room. A woman, seated beside a table near a window, looked up. She had the body of a houri and a delicate, lovely face as impersonally cold as an ascetic's, accented by brooding, violet eyes under fine black brows.

Ewing's excitement made speech hard. "Inez . . . I saw one. Right out there in the street. Just rode by."

She spoke as though from another world. "Saw who?"

"One of *them*—one of Quantrell's men!"

Her sewing dropped and her body stiffened. Her full lips parted. Her hands clenched until the knuckles showed white. Now her voice vibrated like a gong. "You must kill him. Blood for blood! Life for life!"

Her face disintegrated and tears streamed.

Ewing's arm hovered over her shoulder in a second's uncertainty and then gently encircled her. His lips flattened. "Yes, Inez . . . Yes!"

But first, his brain coldly ordered, learn more about this man . . . and the others. Kill . . . but do not be killed in turn.

II

Florence belied its appearance of barely clinging to life on the banks of the Gila. This barren land needed only water to produce, and the river flowed right at hand. The newcomers were given help in making smooth their settling and adjusting. Within a week, every man had an offer of work.

Wayne and Abbie, with Frank and Jesse, scouted the land up and down the river. They would roll the soil between their fingers, noting how the water enriched and gave it body. They finally picked on the most likely area, planning to build their houses fairly near each other for mutual protection in case of Indian raids.

With occasional help from the Burruds, Wayne erected an adobe in the manner of the country, a place where Abbie would feel secure. Only then did he consider several jobs offered to him. His immediate need was cash. Steady work for a few months would remove the pinch and there was much he could do in spare time to clear his land.

Frank and Jesse agreed to watch over Abbie, so early one morning Wayne went to Canby Tryon's loading dock where the bustling little man checked half a dozen big freight wagons headed for the mines. Lew Kearney, already a week on the payroll, introduced him to Canby. "Here's a man can handle horses."

Canby demanded, chin jutting out, "Ever done freighting before?"

"None."

Canby considered Wayne, his shoulders, chest and arms. "Git in the office. I'll talk when I get these wagons off."

He wheeled away and Lew, with a pleased grin, walked off toward his wagon. Wayne went into the office where a tall, blond girl worked at one of the two desks. He took a straight-back chair. He could hear the voices of the teamsters and the crack of whips as, one by one, the wagons rolled out onto the street and away. He became aware that the girl covertly watched him. Several times she bit the end of the pen with white, firm teeth.

"You—you're one of the men who came to Florence with Lew—Mr. Kearney?"

"That's right."

She turned to the ledger and became exceedingly busy. A pretty girl, Wayne thought, but not a candle to Abbie. Tryon bustled in to his desk. He sat down with an explosive sigh, looked at Wayne, fat lips pursed. "So, you can handle horses?"

"All my life, one way or another."

"Friend of Lew Kearney? Another of those damn Johnny Rebs?"

"Another of 'em . . . for four years. Any objections?"

"Plenty! This whole country is overrun with Rebels . . . can't hire anyone else."

Wayne stood up. "Do you want to hire a teamster? Four years of fighting gave me a bellyful and it's over and done. I don't aim to fight it again."

"Pop!" Lorain Tryon cautioned.

Canby grunted. "Sit down. Touchy, like all the rest of 'em!"

In ten minutes Wayne was hired, though not without a crusty word now and then. Wayne now understood Lew's grin. Canby Tryon barked and fizzed but it was meaningless. He painted the job in the worst light—long trips with heavy loads, blasting heat in summer, the ever-present problems of water and the Indians, chance encounters with stray renegades or bands of outlaws. The next morning, Wayne's wagon was one of three that started the journey to the mines in the mountains.

When he received his first pay, Wayne insisted that Abbie get a new dress. He brought her into town early one Saturday, hitched the team before the general store and helped her down. They turned to face Skip Adams, skull face alight. They exchanged news, learning Skip built a house for a merchant at the edge of town.

"And there's more waiting after that," he added.

"Hear you're freighting now, Wayne. Vic Hays got a job riding shotgun for the express company. Luckiest thing we ever did, coming here."

They talked some more before Skip walked on. Wayne left Abbie at the store while he crossed the dusty street and pushed open the batwings of the Gila Saloon. It was comparatively cool in the saloon. Drumbo, Grayson and Joel Ramsey sat at a table near the door, with a bottle before them.

Bed Drumbo turned. His sleeves were rolled high on his muscular arms and there was a sooty smear on one cheek. He waved Wayne to the table. "Sit and pour a drink. We've been talking about you."

Grayson and Joel made room and Wayne sat down. Talk flowed, easy and friendly. Hayes was out on a run, Wayne learned. Hal Grayson now lived above the livery stable where he worked, but he was already starting to horse-trade on the side.

Wayne listened, eyes moving idly about the room. The door at the rear partially opened and a woman appeared, standing tall and silent. Blouse and long, full skirt were widow's black, relieved by bands of white at collar and wrists. The dress could not conceal the mature, full curves of her slender body.

Looking at her face, Wayne had the fascinated impression that he looked on a lifeless mask, each feature frozen in perfect beauty. Only the slight turn of her head gave a semblance of life. Then her eyes—violet, deep and brooding—rested on him. Wayne, shocked, sensed a tortured, imprisoned soul. Then she moved and the door closed.

The man behind the bar came to the table, wiping his hands on his big apron. "Bottle holding out, gents?" His attention centered on Wayne. "I don't think you've been in before. I'm Ewing Vance . . . own this place."

He pushed out his hand. Strong fingers held Wayne's in a powerful grip and then Vance pulled out a chair. "Don't mind if I rest my feet a minute? It's getting so I never get a chance any more. The town's sure growing fast. I can tell it."

Joel Ramsey's china blue eyes grew eager. But Vance had turned to Wayne. "Didn't you come to Florence with these gents? . . . I thought so. I never forget a face. You're always welcome at the Gila."

"Thanks, but a freighter doesn't have much time."

"You're still mighty welcome. I'd say you were a soldier . . . and mighty recently." He glanced at the others. "All of you, for that matter."

"Four years. Too long—and wasted time."

Vance seemed not to notice the subtle withdrawal of the others. He easily rambled on. Gradually, the others joined in, melting under his friendliness. Wayne again saw the woman in the doorway. She stood motionless, arms tightly folded, face immobile. The strange eyes met his for a second then slowly moved away.

Just then, the batwings swung open and the two Burruds came in, Frank leading. Jesse loudly called a surprised greeting and they came to the table as a sudden movement at the distant door caught Wayne's attention. The woman had stepped back within the room and now she peered through a narrow crack of the closing door. Her lips moved convulsively and the next moment the door shut with a soft thud.

Ewing Vance came immediately to his feet, making the Burruds welcome. He brought another bottle. "This one's on me—a welcome to strangers who I hope will become friends. If you want to talk private, let me know."

They murmured protests and that was enough for Vance. He remained at the table, now talking about Florence and its dreams of a golden future. "Everyone of you has work—and a year ago there was practically nothing here."

Joel shook his head. "All but me, and you've got the only saloon in town."

"You're a barman?"

"My trade—before the war. I tended bar—well, lots of places."

Vance leaned on the table, his cheeks sucked in as his eyes swung from man to man, back to Joel. He threw a hasty look over his shoulder toward the distant door, then came to a decision. “The place is more than one man can handle and I’ve been looking for someone I can trust.”

Frank Burrud spoke up. “Joel’s your man.”

Vance smacked his hand on the table. “Good! When can you start?”

Joel came to his feet. “Now.”

Vance untied his apron and tossed it to Joel. “Why, so you can. Drinks around—on me. It’ll be pure pleasure to see someone else behind the bar.”

Joel strode away, to return with filled shot-glasses that he dexterously placed around the table. His mild eyes glowing, he returned to the bar to familiarize himself with the stock.

Ewing Vance settled back in his chair with a sigh. Frank Burrud spoke with quiet enthusiasm of the progress on the farm and Bedford Drumbo glanced up at the clock. “That horse still needs a shoe, but I reckon I can spare the time. There’s no sergeant kicking my rump.”

“Another soldier,” Vance cut in. “I bet all of you saw service—maybe the same outfit.”

Frank gravely asked, “Now what gave you that idea?”

“You all came to Florence together. It makes a man think you served together.”

Wayne laughed. “Up to when we met on the trail, I never saw these men.”

Burrud agreed. “That’s right. All of us fought—

some in Virginia, some in Tennessee, some down in Mississippi. We just happened to meet."

Wayne caught Vance's flicker of disbelief as he turned the conversation to the war in general. The others listened, but the pleasure of the gathering had dissipated. Vance mentioned the Missouri-Kansas border and the fighting in Arkansas. Jesse Burrud studied his drink with a frowning concentration. Bed Drumbo looked uneasily at the clock and Grayson made rings on the table with the bottom of his glass.

"Friend of mine," Ewing Vance continued, apparently oblivious of the tension, "happened to be around Lawrence when Quantrell's men hit the town. These damned Yanks got exactly what they deserved."

Drumbo sat frozen, brows drawn, and Grayson stopped fiddling with his glass. The skin drew tight over his pronounced cheekbones and his mouth tightened into a thin, pale line.

Frank sighed, eyes haunted. "Who hasn't heard of Lawrence? It was a wrong and horrid thing."

"To destroy a Yank nest like that!" Vance laughed scathingly. "Hell! You talk like a Yank yourself! I hear they want to find everyone of those raiders and string 'em up."

Burrud said, "None of us are Yanks. But no decent man would excuse that renegade, Quantrell. As for hanging all of them—no, I don't agree. There were some who didn't know what they were in for when they joined him."

"Were you there?"

"It's best forgotten."

Grayson slapped his empty glass on the table. "You're right, Frank. I need another drink."

The conversation veered away. Vance studied each man, his eyes lingering longest on Bedford Drumbo. More customers came in and Vance finally left the table to help Joel Ramsey behind the bar. Wayne glanced at the high wall clock and hastily excused himself. Abbie would have had time to buy a dozen dresses. He invited the Burruds some evening for supper and left the saloon.

He pulled his hat brim low against the blinding sun and hurried toward the store, certain Abbie would be waiting. He passed the marshal's adobe office and jail but swung around when he heard his name called. Hank Malloy came out, his badge a bright glitter against the worn black of his open vest. He was a man in his early forties; stocky, square-faced, brown eyes placid. A thick, mouse-brown mustache broadened and fleshed his nose. He was a bull-strong, plodding man, tenacious and stubborn.

He shifted a chewed match to one corner of his lips and pushed back his hat with the tip of a broad thumb. "You heading for Canby's? Tell him the Apaches are kicking up trouble again."

"Around here!"

"Not yet, but they travel fast and far and we're close to the Apache Trail out of the Superstitions. Best you and the other drivers take along extra rifles and ammunition."

"They'll hit Florence?"

Hank considered that for a long moment. "Don't think so—too big a place for their liking. But mines, freight wagons and stage coaches is something else. Best keep a sharp eye."

Wayne thanked him, suddenly worried. Maybe the Apaches would not be bold enough to attack the town, but he wondered about two new adobe houses on the bank of the river. He stopped at Canby's and passed the news. The little man glared at Wayne as though he had something to do with the Indians. "I'll have extra weapons and bullets. Those damn Apaches! Trickier than Confederates . . . and that's going some!"

Wayne grinned tightly. He had grown used to Canby's peppery way but the man's constant, scathing remarks about the Lost Cause still irritated him.

He found Abbie at the store, talking to Lorain Tryon. Abbie had to display the dress she bought, then Wayne loaded the wagon while she had a few last words with Lorain. They left the town behind them and Wayne let the horses set their own pace. Abbie was filled with woman-talk and Wayne half-listened contentedly, his mind on the group at the Gila Saloon and, particularly, Ewing

Vance. He wondered why there was something vaguely disturbing about the man. He suddenly became aware of Abbie's talk.

"What was that?—about Lew Kearney?"

"You haven't been listening! I think something will happen between him and Lorain Tryon."

"Now what makes you think that!"

"It's plain enough—to a woman. Lorain asks a question about him as though it's not important but she listens close enough. He's taken her eye. I can tell it. Have you noticed?"

"Come to think of it, he finds reasons to be in the office more'n the rest of us."

"There! You see?"

Wayne smiled. "They'd make a nice pair."

"Yes, but don't count chickens. Canby Tryon'd fair blow up if he knew his daughter is interested in a Johnny Reb."

"Canby could get a lot worse son-in-law, though."

"Well, Lew will have a mighty long, hard pull."

Wayne clucked to the horses and slapped the reins over their sleek rumps.

Back at the Gila Saloon, a steady stream of customers kept Ewing and Joel busy. Often, Vance looked at the table and the six men. His eyes would darken briefly, then clear as he looked quickly away. He suddenly snapped off his apron, said shortly, "Take care of the bar."

Joel nodded in mild surprise. Vance walked to the closed door at the rear. He tapped lightly then pushed it open, disappeared inside. The door closed with a dull thud. He leaned against it, took a deep breath and exhaled with a long sigh. Inez sat at a table on which stood an ornate lamp. She held a picture in her lap, hypnotically staring at it.

A pained expression crossed Vance's face. The picture, at first glance, might be taken for him. Clear eyes, set wide apart, held an other-worldly light. There were the same almost bloodless lips, the straight, lank hair brushed back in a wave from a pale forehead. His brother's face—mouldering now in a Lawrence graveyard, he thought savagely. His hand hovered over Inez', then lightly touched her.

She looked up. He was startled by the naked savagery in her violet eyes, the animal curl of her full lips. "One of them—out there—"

Her voice choked and Vance asked quickly, "Yes?"

"He was there when they—murdered my husband." She lifted the picture and her face convulsed as she placed it on the table and angrily twisted from under his hand. She whirled around the table to a sideboard, jerked open a drawer and her hand darted inside. The gun glittered as she turned.

Vance jumped between her and the door, his

fingers circling her wrist, pushing the weapon aside and down. "Inez! What are you doing!"

"I'll kill him—like he killed Edward!"

"Inez!"

He snatched the weapon from her. Firmly but gently, he forced her down into a chair. She looked up at him in amazed horror. "You—you'd let him get away!"

He knelt beside her and cupped her hands in his. His voice became soothing. "Wait, Inez. It'll come in due time. I recognized another one, remember? I think there's a whole bunch of them here. I'll find out." He turned his head toward the barroom. "That's why I hired that son of a bitch. I'll pump him. We won't move until we know."

"A—bunch of them?"

"Nine, at least. But we have to make sure."

Her face twisted out of its cameo loveliness. "Nine! Here? Given into our hands? Ewing, I'll help you kill all of them."

He stroked her hand until tension left her. Finally he walked to the door, looked back at the beautiful woman at the table. He felt a chill, something like fear, and shook it off. He wondered if he had ever known Inez and the dark things that came out of the depths of her mind. He fixed a smile on his face and opened the door.

She had a right to hate—as he did. It was her husband and his brother who had died at

Lawrence. Who could blame him or Inez for hatred after that inferno of horror?

He shook off the new chill as he approached the bar and sang out a hearty greeting to a customer.

III

Hatred acted as a spur and indecision as a checkrein on Ewing Vance. In exhausted torment, he cursed the day that nine men and a woman had ridden into Florence. Hatred brought him to the very brink of a chasm and fiercely urged him to jump. But he knew that once he struck the first blow, there could be no turning back. He would exult in this chance to become an avenging sword and then draw back in horror from the thought of cold, deliberate murder.

So he blew hot and cold, became morose and withdrawn. Twice he took the loaded Peacemaker from under the bar and then slowly replaced it. The Lord alone claimed vengeance . . . but the Lord used human agents as his tools! Hadn't Ewing promised Inez time and again that if he ever encountered one of Quantrell's raiders, that man would die?

She urged him on, more subtly and more powerfully than by word or act. She sat with Edward's picture, or he became aware of her brooding eyes following him, silently asking a question, pressing upon him the necessity for an answer. She built a wall of silence that grew day by day until Ewing felt that the very air vibrated with it.

He deliberately relived that day when guerrilla rifles and pistols wantonly murdered men around him and he felt the smash of the bullet along his own skull. The scar was still there, under his hair. He lashed himself with the knowledge that one of the murderers worked in his saloon and another came each day to rinse the soot of the smithy out of his throat.

And there were seven more! He had learned this from Joel Ramsey. The nine men had come together, along with Abbie Nelson, and they stuck together. To mention Lawrence was to see their faces grow secretive as they exchanged warning glances. They were Quantrell's men, everyone of them. Outlaws, they had fled, and the law that could touch them was far away, for Hank Malloy would have no authority. Who, then, could blame Ewing Vance for exacting justice?

So he brought himself to the very brink of action, only to face that inner barrier still strong enough to stay him. The intensity of the silent battle would sometimes drive him away from Inez' brooding, accusing silence, out of the sight of Joel Ramsey's unsuspecting, ready laughter, away from Bedford Drumbo at the bar, a whiskey glass in his hand.

As tonight—he had again visited the rambling adobe at the edge of town, where the blinds were always pulled and the door always open to men who felt the need for Madam Verona's hospitality.

Now he walked down the hall to the parlor with its gilt chairs and deep red velvet drapes, leaving Fern Eccles in the room behind him. Madam Verona, alone, glanced up from a solitaire layout and gathered up the cards with a bored sigh.

"Sit a spell, Ewing. I'm yawning my head off." She gestured with a bare, plump arm toward a sideboard on which bottles and glasses sat. "We could have a couple of drinks."

Vance fidgeted in the doorway a moment and then, with a shrug, picked up a bottle, dropped into a chair across the table.

"Your health." Madam Verona downed her drink with a quick, practiced toss, genteelly patted her lips with a square of linen and lace. She noticed he still held his full glass. "Drink up, man!"

He gave her a twist of a smile and drank half the liquor. Madam Verona studied him. She was a big-bosomed woman in her forties, still striking, though time thickened her chin and neck, put fine traceries in her full cheeks under the rice powder. She wore a velvet evening gown that exposed a great expanse of shoulder and breasts. Her eyes were bright and shrewd. Madam Verona, like many of her kind, was generous but no fool.

Now she judged Vance's mood, chose the rumor of Apache trouble as a safe topic. She rambled on and gradually Vance eased into his chair and finished his drink.

Fern Eccles, an over-plump china figurine of a woman with empty blue eyes and a vacuous smile, came in. Madam caught Vance's irritated stir and she waved the girl away. She filled Vance's glass again.

It was always easy to talk here, easy to drink and gossip with Madam Verona, kid with the girls, or share earthy jokes with the men in the cozy fraternity of the place. No chance word would bring regret and the shadow of horror was dispelled.

He gradually warmed and laughed aloud at some incident and Madam Verona chuckled. Perhaps a slow and boring evening pushed her on. She studied him, still smiling. "I guess I know about every secret in the town—and a hell of a distance around."

Ewing laughed wryly. "Anyone comes here has a secret if he didn't before."

"True enough, Ewing. But there's one I've never been able to figure out."

"What?" he asked, reaching for the bottle.

"You."

His hand froze, his eyes grew suddenly cold. Then he laughed and poured his drink. "Me? Hell, this is my only secret!"

"But why? I've seen your wife. A man with a woman that beautiful stays home, but you come here."

His lips grew more bloodless than ever. He was

startled and upset and she instantly called herself a fool for breaking one of her cardinal rules. She forced a chuckle. "Forget it, Ewing."

"Sure," he said shortly but his eyes never left her. Then he arose. "All men wander, I guess. Maybe that's it."

She did not try to keep him, knowing that once this incident had passed and lost its sharpness he would be back. Vance picked up his hat and slipped out of the front door. He stood a moment, looking towards the lights of the town. Then he strode away from them. A movement and sound behind him caused him to turn.

Madam Verona's door opened, throwing its square of light on a muscular, short figure. Vance recognized Bed Drumbo. One of them! His teeth clenched against the inner turmoil Madam Verona had aroused. He turned away, strode blindly, not caring where his feet took him. He saw the starlit glint of water ahead and below. He stopped, looking across the river to the black line of the low hills, hearing the river's mysterious whisper.

A scathing inner voice mocked. Why didn't you tell Madam Verona? You married a beautiful woman who, as Edward once told you, could blaze with passion. Now she's yours in the way of the law but you can't break the cold shell of a dead love. Once or twice you thought you had but, afterwards, you knew it was Edward she held in her arms. So you go to Madam Verona's—to the passive, pallid substitutes for the fire and passion you need.

A new voice asked, Could vengeance lay the ghost? If nine men died, would the near-madness that seized Inez at Lawrence disappear—and Edward with it?

He beat his fist in his palm, glaring at the ghostly, rippling waters, then up at the cold, impersonal stars. His mind whirled him back in a kaleidoscope of pictures.

He could see Lawrence again; the streets, the houses and stores; the finger-lift of the church steeple into the sky. In the fateful fall of '63, Ewing had gone there to visit Edward. It had been three years since they had met, for Edward had accepted the pulpit at Lawrence, met Inez and married her while Ewing had remained on his father's Kentucky farm. When the old man died, Ewing took the roundabout trip to Kansas, daring the uncertainty of the campaigns in Missouri and Arkansas.

His heart had jumped at the first sight of Inez. He forced himself to hide his blaze of desire from her and Edward, who was now a chaplain to a Union regiment. Even more, he had helped hundreds of runaway slaves from Missouri and Arkansas, so he was hated by the Rebels probably more than any other man in Kansas. Edward was always the idealist, the one with a cause. He thundered at Vance to fight for the Lord, to join a new regiment forming in Lawrence.

Vance closed his eyes now as he remembered the worshiping look in Inez' face as she listened, spellbound. Edward had owned her—body, brain, and soul! The thought seared through Vance as he paced in aimless, tortured steps. What a ghastly travesty of that his own marriage was.

The vivid pictures returned. Under Edward's urgings and, really, to gain favor with Inez, he had taken the army oath. On a November evening he and the other unarmed volunteers camped in the town square and Edward fervently prayed for their triumph and safety. At that very moment, Quantrell's Raiders, three or four hundred strong, took position about the town under the cover of darkness.

Vance stood quite still now on the bank of the dark river as he lived those hours again. How bright with sun and promise that morning had been! The recruits had just finished breakfast when they heard the wild rebel yell. Riders out of nowhere charged down the street. Vance glimpsed wild, distorted faces, heard the thunder of hoofs and the crash of guns. A man ran from the hotel. A saber flashed in the sun and the man fell dead.

Before the recruits could gather their wits, the raiders were upon them. Some of the recruits fled but most of them milled until, with deadly precision, they were forced into the center of a ring of black gun muzzles staring into their faces. Vance and his companions were helpless. He heard the thunder of rifle fire, hoarse shouts, frightened yells and screams. Flames crackled and smoke lifted into the bright sky. Vance saw sprawled forms lying in the street, saw the raiders scatter through the town in a lust of killing, looting, and burning.

A man pulled his horse to a plunging, rearing halt, barked a command and indicated the helpless prisoners. The guards' rifles and revolvers leveled. Vance had a split second of horrified realization before darts of flame and a roaring thunder swept over him. He had a flashing explosion within his head.

There was the sound of voracious flames and the acrid bite of smoke when his eyes opened again. He was the only one of the group alive, for the bullet had but cut a deep groove along his skull. The raiders were gone.

He pulled himself up and he thought of Inez—then Edward. He was not certain how he managed to reach their house. It was undamaged, serene and aloof from the outside. But the moment he stepped into the open doorway, the illusion shattered.

Edward lay dead in a pool of blood, a dozen bullets in his body. Inez sat beside him, swaying, eyes glazed, face dull. She didn't look up, couldn't speak, didn't know Vance.

In the confusion of the next few days, no one remembered that Vance had been sworn into the army and Inez, still helpless in shock, needed him. With Edward dead, Vance did not intend to lose her. She moved in a numb, nightmare world and Vance took charge. He took her back to his farm in Kentucky.

She remained in shock for the whole of the journey, hardly speaking, obeying automatically, barely seeing the world about her. Once on the farm, though, she gradually came out of the paralysis. But she lived as if she must patiently wait for death.

For a long time Vance despaired of her. But his love kept him grimly at the task and, bit by bit, she approached normalcy. He told her then that he loved her and wanted to marry her. Edward was gone now and she was alone.

"Edward is dead?" she had repeated, staring at him with those great violet eyes. The first, despairing realization of it crushed her and in a horror of amazed disbelief Vance heard her keening cry. Shock had blocked off reality from her and his own words had, in a sense, murdered Edward a second time.

She had gone into delirium and high fever. When Vance knew death would take her, the fever broke and the delirium left. A month later he again proposed and she accepted as though nothing really mattered. They were married—and his own house of dreams shattered. She performed all her duties. She depended on him. She never crossed him; she obeyed as a slave would a master.

That was all. He took her, but she was not there—a quiescent body from which the soul had departed. Vance's ardor vanished and he cursed his brother. But the ghost could not be exorcised. Maybe a move would change things. In despair and anger, Ewing sold the farm and struck out for the West. For a time Inez did show more interest, had more life. Once she had responded to him with the passion and fierceness that he knew she possessed. It had happened after they came to Florence and he had opened the Gila Saloon. Now he knew her ecstasy had been for a dead man. The old fears and ghosts returned and she lived more and more within herself.

Ewing sighed deeply in the night. A man should not live in such hell. But he loved her! Enough to take the husk if he could have nothing else.

He walked with a weary stride, shoulders hunched. He could only continue to hope and again he damned Lawrence, Quantrell's Raiders and the twisted thing they had made of his life. He had sworn a fierce blood covenant that if he ever met with one of those killers, that man would die.

Well, he had the chance now—nine chances. He stopped short, looking toward the dim light above Madam Verona's door. Their coming had aroused Inez. She wanted vengeance and he had not seen her so alive since Lawrence.

Bedford Drumbo—the man's face had been one of those indelibly printed on his mind that early morning in Lawrence. Drumbo had been one of the guards about the volunteers, one of the executioners.

What had Inez said? "God has put them in your hands to send them to the hell waiting for them. Maybe Edward could rest then."

In hope and despair he sensed a promise. Up to now he had hesitated, but if the nine died—one at a time—then their blood would exorcise Edward's ghost. Inez could turn to him as a wife.

Ewing bit his fisted knuckles, still staring at the distant light. If Madam Verona could even half guess his secret! If he struck and struck again with the cunning of a serpent, he would no longer need women like Fern Eccles. And Bedford Drumbo even now dallied in the house behind that light!

His hand dropped and his shoulders squared. He hurried home. When he eased open the kitchen door, he could hear the muted noise from the saloon in the front part of the building. He stood quiet, senses probing for Inez.

He heard a slight stir and knew that she

turned in the bed. Satisfied, he moved through the darkness with complete familiarity to the sideboard. But an inner voice cautioned him as his groping fingers touched the gun.

He returned to the kitchen and, from a wall rack above the work table, drew a heavy, long-bladed knife. He touched the point, turned to the door and eased into the night again.

Less than an hour later, Bedford Drumbo stepped out of Madam Verona's house. He called back a coarse joke, his stocky figure clearly revealed in the light. He laughed and turned away as someone closed the door and he became hardly more than a heavy shadow.

Another shadow flitted after, closing the distance. A dog barked afar off and the stars looked coldly down as the shadows suddenly merged. There was a swift, fierce flurry, a glint of starlight on steel and a choked, gurgling, strangling cry.

The night fell into silence except for the distant, persistent and mournful bark of the dog.

IV

Once the two wagons had made the steep grade up from the river, Wayne Nelson looked back to make sure Lew Kearney would have no trouble with the slope. Satisfied, Wayne settled again and his whistle lifted above the rumble of the wheels and the creak of the wagon. Far to the north, he could see the distant blue suggestion of the Superstitions. The horizon was unmarred by smoke signal or dust cloud. Apaches still kicked up trouble but mainly to the south. Yet who could ever know where they would appear?

His whistle stopped as, looking eastward, he saw several circling black specks against the sky. They dropped below the hills, but two more appeared out of nowhere against the bright blue, only to disappear in turn. He frowned, judging they were several miles out in this desert-jungle of saguaro.

He slapped the reins against sleek rumps and clucked at the horses. His eyes moved back to the sky but it was empty now. Big animal, maybe a horse or a cow. Wouldn't pay a man to leave the wagon and stray off afoot that far just to find out which. He dismissed it and his whistle lifted again.

The steady pace of the two wagons continued

until the sun climbed high overhead. When Wayne could not see the horses' shadows to either side, he pulled off the road, reined the horses in. A few moments later Lew Kearney pulled in behind him. They adjusted nose bags on the horses, built a small fire for chow and coffee.

They ate. Then Wayne remembered what Abbie had said and he threw a sidelong glance at Lew. "How about you and Lorain Tryon?"

"How'd you know?"

"Abbie says it's plain to see."

"And I thought I hid it pretty well!"

Lew made idle tracery in the sand, glanced uncertainly at Wayne. Then, as though he ached to talk, he broke into a flood of eager words. He was in love with Lorain. He had to be near her, he found a dozen excuses to look at her as she worked at her desk. Not, he admitted with a pleased smile, that she never looked his way, too. There was something electric between them and Lew knew the girl felt it as much as he did.

Then his face fell. "But there ain't much hope of getting anywhere."

Wayne nodded. "Canby, I reckon. Said anything to her?"

"Can't. A couple of times I worked up nerve to speak more'n just the time of day, but she always cut me off with a sign and a look at her paw. He'd fire me in a minute if he learned I even looked at his daughter. Not that I couldn't get another job, but this'n keeps me close to her."

Wayne stood up and brushed sand from the seat of his levis. "It's a mean problem. What are you going to do?"

Lew sighed, face drawn. "I don't know—I just purely don't!"

Wayne jerked his hat lower over his eyes. "We'd best be getting on. There's a lot of miles to cover."

Back in the town, Ewing Vance worked the rag over the zinc-topped bar for the twentieth time. The big room was dark compared to the blinding sun on the dusty street beyond the batwings. He heard an ambling clop-clop of a horse and his hand stilled. The lazy sound grew louder, then faded. Ewing moistened his lips and continued to polish the bar. The big room was empty, the door to the living quarters closed. He had an impulse to tell Inez. He decided against it. Not yet . . . wait and see. He looked at the clock. Sooner or later, they'd find out and he wished to hell they'd make the discovery.

The batwings swung open and Ewing's eyes cut to them, tense yet eager. Hank Malloy came to the bar, removing his hat and wiping his forehead. He ordered a drink, leaned heavily against the bar. Ewing waited a moment. "A quiet day?"

"Not even a dog in the road!"

"Any sign of Apaches?"

Hank tossed off his drink. "Nary a one. Of course, might be the cavalry is out this way. That'd drive 'em off."

"Sure hope it does. I'd hate to hear someone around here fell in their hands."

"Amen to that, Vance!"

Hank left and again silence settled on the room. Ewing pursed his lips, considering the thought he had placed in the lawman's mind. No slip here, he decided. It came up naturally. He braced himself against the drag of time.

He took a broom out on the porch. He casually looked up at a clear, unsullied sky. He walked to the rear of the building where he could see the low sweep of the hills to the north and east.

Then he saw them! Small, dark specks off beyond the river. Buzzards! He saw them drop out of sight, one by one. He could picture what happened out there in a desolate fold of the hills and his stomach made a slow, heaving turn. Then his face smoothed and he walked back into the saloon.

Just before noon, Joel Ramsey came in, spoke cheerily and tied his apron around his ample waist. Ewing made a sour comment about the lack of business and went through the rear door to the lunch that Inez had waiting for him. It was a silent meal. He returned to the saloon, edgy, and was relieved to see Canby Tryon seated alone at a table. Ewing joined him.

A few moments later Hal Grayson pushed open the batwings. The big Viking of a man looked briefly around and then went to the bar. "Joel, I'm looking for Bed. Seen him around?"

"Ain't been in since I come on. Mr. Vance, you seen him?"

Ewing held his voice steady and casual. "Not since yesterday."

Hal Grayson frowned. "Funny. He didn't show up for work."

"Maybe Drumbo had a big evening." Vance scratched his head. "Asked at Madam Verona's?"

Grayson's face cleared. "Maybe that's it. You can never tell about Bed when he's drinking."

"Never could," Joel agreed and Grayson left.

Ewing considered Joel, a strange light in his eyes. "You and Bed are old friends?"

"For a long time."

"And Grayson? All those you come to town with?"

Joel frowned. "Why do you ask, Mr. Vance?"

Ewing chuckled. "Too polite to ask *them,* I guess. Every one of you served in the War?"

"Yes," Joel answered curtly, cutting off further questions.

Ewing was satisfied. He waved goodbye as Canby Tryon left. Three more men came in, then another. Ewing glanced at the clock. He felt more assured now but he'd like to get this business over. By mid-afternoon the bar and the room hummed with talk. They heard the pistol-like crack of the whip as the Tucson stage rolled in, distant shouts and calls. The noise stopped for a moment and then picked up again.

Ewing looked up as the batwings swung to admit three or four men, one of them Vic Hayes. He still wore his cartridge-studded belt and holstered gun. He ordered a drink. Like Grayson, Vic was tall and blond but he had a breadth of shoulder and depth of chest that made him appear stocky rather than tall. In some long-past fight, Hayes had gained a broken nose. He downed his drink, expelled his breath with a pleased sigh.

"That's a long and dusty run from Tucson!" He sobered. "Joel, I hear Bed's missing."

Joel paused in the act of opening a bottle. "Ain't he showed up yet?"

"Nope. Hal asked all over town and finally saddled up and rode toward the river. Figured Bed might be at the Burruds' or the Nelsons'."

Joel shrugged. "Hal will find him. You know how Bed does."

Vic nodded, though plainly unconvinced. He had another drink, joining in the talk around the bar. Ewing smiled and glanced toward the door in the rear. It was partially open and he knew Inez had been listening. Her deep eyes turned to him and he read the question in them. He deliberately turned his back and the door closed.

The sun was westering when there was a disturbance in the street. The batwings burst open and a man pushed his head in the room and yelled, “They found Drumbo! Looks like Apaches!”

There was a concerted rush to the door. Vic Hayes leading. Joel dropped a glass, raced around the end of the bar. Though prepared for this all day, Ewing’s legs and arms trembled and his knees wanted to give way. He took a deep breath, fighting for control.

At last he joined the group on the porch, stood on tiptoe to look over heads. Hal Grayson, straight and grim-faced, walked by. He led his own horse and, draped over the saddle, was a bloody shape that had once been a body. A ribbon of torn cloth waved in the gentle breeze that now stirred out of the west.

Everywhere along the street shocked people watched but did not move or speak. Grayson walked with a steady rhythm, like a man in a nightmare. He and his grim burden turned in at the marshal’s office.

No one came back into the bar with Ewing and he was thankful. He grabbed a bottle and poured a drink, spilling some of the whiskey. He downed it, stood with eyes closed, waiting the bite, the spread of new courage through his body. He opened his eyes.

Inez again stood in the doorway and their eyes locked. Hers shifted to the batwings, back to him. He found his voice. "You heard?"

"Who?"

"Bedford Drumbo. I—"

Men streamed in and Inez hastily closed the door. Ewing forced himself to work the bar. The men were shocked by what they had seen and only by gesture did they order whiskey and down it in a horrified silence. Then, almost as one, they broke into speech. Ewing served them, took another drink himself.

The batwings flew wide. Hank Malloy, Vic Hayes and Joel came in. Hal Grayson, looking pale, strained, and sick, was with them. Hank's square jaw was set and his mustache bristled. He pushed men aside and shoved Grayson to the bar.

"This man needs a drink—bad. Leave him alone until he's had it."

Joel joined Ewing behind the bar, round face set, china blue eyes enormous. He poured for Hayes, Hank, and Grayson, then one for himself. Grayson pushed his empty to Joel. "Another," he said in a trembling voice, shuddered. "I don't know how in hell I managed to bring him in!"

Gradually, as Hal recovered, the story came out. He had looked everywhere for Drumbo, then struck out along the river. He had been ready to give up when he saw buzzards lift over the hills on the other side of the Gila. "They flew lazy and drunk, like they were stuffed. I—something just told me, so I went over to look around. I found him."

He closed his eyes and gripped the bar. Hank Malloy took up the story. "Apaches got him. They have a special way of mutilating a man. We can tell their work. Then the buzzards took over. If it wasn't for what's left of his clothes and what was in his pockets, you'd never know it was Drumbo."

Ewing asked, "But what was Drumbo doing clean over there?"

Vic Hayes glowered. "I don't think Bed went over there. He'd do some funny things when he was drinking . . . if he was . . . but he wouldn't wander that far out in the desert. He was taken."

Ewing's back grew cold and suddenly his palms sweat. Then he realized Hayes had been many miles away last night. "I don't see how you figure it."

"Apaches! They were sneaking around the edge of town and Bed was out late—alone. They took him out there and—or maybe they killed him here and did the rest of the job in the hills."

"My God!" Ewing exclaimed. He ordered Joel to pour drinks around, seized his own and downed it. Relief and triumph flooded through him. He turned to the marshal. "Hank, if the red devils are this close, you'd better send for the cavalry. No one will be safe."

A murmur ran through the group but Hank slapped his hand on the bar. "Now wait a minute! All of us know damn well Apaches don't fight at night. They're afraid of ghosts!"

Ewing looked skeptical. "But Vic makes sense."

"I ain't saying Apaches didn't do this. But Drumbo probably wandered off last night and slept it off along the river bank. Some wandering Indians came on him early this morning. They took him up in the hills."

An argument started but Ewing saw that most of them agreed with Hank, too fearful to consider the other alternative. He signaled Joel to take care of the bar. He eased out of the crowd and went to the living quarters.

Inez stepped back from the door when he entered. He did not move as he faced his wife. She studied him, searching his face, a bright new light in her eyes. Her full breasts lifted with her gusty breathing.

Her voice whispered, "I heard you come in and go out last night. It was a long time before you came back."

He said nothing, eyes devouring her. Her voice became more throaty. "I can't find the shirt and pants you wore yesterday."

He spoke flatly. "One of Quantrell's Raiders is dead . . . Drumbo."

"I heard. It wasn't Apaches?"

"No. I buried the clothing this side of the river. Blood."

Her eyes deepened and then came alight. Her clenched hands half lifted in a gesture of triumph. Then they opened and her arms extended to him as he stepped forward. She pressed against him, fingers digging into his back. Her whisper came, choked, quivering. "Ah, you're proving to be a man! I knew!"

He groped behind him, threw the bolt on the door. Then he swept her up in his arms, looked questioningly at her. Her violet eyes blazed and she fiercely pressed her lips against his.

He carried her to the other room.

V

Now spring was on the desert—that too-fleeting time when browns, beiges and dusty greens are enlivened by riots of yellows, reds and softly bright pastels. The days were pleasant, the sky a beneficent blue that all too soon would turn a brassy, iron weight. Returning with empty wagons from the mines, Wayne and Lew were amazed at this new aspect of the drab desert. Even the grim mountains softened under the touch of spring.

They surrendered to the illusion, as all desert dwellers do. The horses moved quickly along and an intermittently complaining wheel seemed to sing instead of screech. Wayne's whistle lifted high and clear. But he sobered, recalling that Bedford Drumbo had missed all this beauty. He had been buried a month now and the Apache excitement had died down.

At their usual nooning, Wayne and Lew talked idly of their next trip and Wayne sighed contentedly. "I won't be making many more runs. I've almost got enough ready money now to give all my time to the farm. Abbie needs me around the place."

Lew said enviously, "Wish I could be with Lorain all the time."

"You've got it bad, boy! Canby doesn't know?"

"We don't see one another often. Lorain and me manage to meet at the depot when he's out of the office. A couple of times we made it at night, she taking a breath of air and me waiting somewhere close in the shadows." Lew made an angry grimace. "I want to ask Canby for permission to see her regular. But Lorain wants we should wait. I'm not certain I can. I fair ache for that girl!"

Wayne touched Lew's arm. "Be patient."

Lew looked away with a gesture of defeat. "You and her argue alike. I guess I can manage to keep from busting."

They reached town late in the afternoon and Wayne hurried to get back to Abbie. The next morning, he hitched up his own wagon, helped Abbie into the high seat, and drove sedately into town. Wayne turned in at the hitchrack of the general store. He and Abbie ordered supplies, then he left her to look at dress material and gewgaws. He walked to that ubiquitous western man's club, the saloon.

There was a large group at one of the tables when he entered the Gila. Frank Burrud and his brother listened gravely to Hayes make vehement points with a finger raised under Hank Malloy's bristling mustache. Cadaverous Skip Adams sat beyond Jesse, slouched in his seat, his skeletal fingers folded across his open black vest. Ewing Vance sat next to Hank, eyes veiled.

As Wayne came up, Hank's jaw set stubbornly. "Vic, you're plain crazy! It was Apaches and no one else killed Bed Drumbo."

Vic impatiently shoved back a lock of corn gold hair. "I know it's what everyone says, but it don't figure."

Ewing called over his shoulder, "Joel, bring another bottle. Wayne Nelson just come in to join the argument." He caught Vic's attention then. "I agree with Hank. There's no other reason for Drumbo being killed how and where he was."

As Wayne pulled up a chair, he glimpsed Inez standing in the open doorway but his attention swung back to the conversation. Vic was saying, "You figure Bed was knocked out at the edge of town but the Apaches finished him over there in the hills. Yet there was no Indian sign around his body and there wasn't any report of 'em within thirty miles of here!"

Hank impatiently stroked his mustache. "Vic, you don't know how tricky Apaches can be. They can be fifty miles away in the morning and trying to knife you that afternoon. They come out of nowhere like a bunch of damn ghosts and they disappear the same way."

Hank lifted a hand as Vic started to protest. "What they did to Drumbo—what we could see after the buzzards got through—was Apache and nothing else."

Wayne looked up just as Inez Vance softly closed the door.

Wayne drove home toward sundown. Abbie was filled with gossip. "I talked to Lorain Canby. To hear her tell it, she's as much in love with Lew Kearney as I am with you. Impossible, of course."

He gave her a squeeze that made her gasp. "I swear, Wayne Nelson, you get rougher every day! Anyhow, I think Lorain has just about worked up courage to talk to her father. Lew is too fine a boy to lose because Canby's a crusty old fire-eater."

It was near dusk when they started supper and Wayne lit the two kitchen lamps. They finished the meal and, while Abbie busied herself about the kitchen, Wayne remained at the table, cutting and patching a broken harness rein. He pulled the lamp closer.

Abbie rattled the dishes as she talked of Lorain and Lew. Wayne listened, knife busy on the leather. A faint breeze came through the open windows and, beyond, the desert stretched in somnolent peace.

Abbie dried a pot, holding it toward the light near the big range as Wayne dropped wearily back in the chair. The bullet sliced the air where his head had been a split second before. The distant crack of the rifle was drowned in the crash of the slug into the stove, its high whine as it ricocheted and thudded into a low ceiling beam. Wayne sat stupefied, Abbie's scream echoing in the room. Then a hot iron creased like a flash across the fleshy part of his forearm and the second bullet thudded into the wall. He heard the muted smack of the rifle.

He jumped up and his breath snuffed out the lamp as Abbie whirled about and blew out the second lamp. Blackness instantly engulfed the room.

Abbie's voice came low and firm. "Wayne! Here's your rifle!"

She shoved it into his hands and he eased to the window. He looked out into the silent desert night. He saw the dull, false-smooth gray of the desert floor and the tall, black shapes and shadows of saguaro. Nothing moved. There was no sound.

Abbie stirred but he flung his hand back, barring her from the window. "Wayne, what is it? Indians?"

"I don't think so. From what I hear, Apaches are afraid of the dark."

Wayne searched the night and his ears strained for sound that did not come. He wondered if sounds of the shots had carried to the Burrud place.

"Who, Wayne?" Abbie insisted.

"I aim to find out. Get my gun belt."

She melted away without question, returning soon with his holstered Colt. He handed her the rifle and hastily buckled on the belt, set the holster to his leg.

He slipped out the door while Abbie took his place at the window with the rifle. Wayne paused in the deep shadow of the house, judging that the ambusher lurked somewhere down by the river. Its sloping bank would make an excellent cover if he waited for Wayne to come after him. It would also afford a shield behind which he could slip away, unseen and unheard.

Either way, a gamble. Wayne cat-footed an erratic course toward the line of tall saguaros. He reached them, stopped to listen, gun in his hand. The night was silent, but the ambusher might be anywhere—or nowhere.

He made a wide circle and ghosted in toward the river bank. He had just reached it when, far behind him, he heard a lifting beat of hoofs along the road. A hoarse shout broke the silence. "Wayne! Abbie! Are you there!"

The Burruds—but Abbie would meet them. The ambusher would have to make a definite play now. Wayne tried to penetrate the tricky shadows along the river, probed for sound above the constant whisper of the current.

He heard voices back at the house but he waited, gun ready. But at last he knew the ambusher had undoubtedly fled after the second unsuccessful shot. He turned back to the house.

The Burruds joined him and they beat circles

about the place without result. Frank and Jesse wanted to stay but Wayne would have nothing of it. "That man would be a fool to come back tonight. He'll know we're waiting for him."

"Who was he?" Frank demanded.

"I don't know. I don't figure it was Apaches, but no one else has any reason to gun for me."

They hazarded a wild guess it might have been a madman or a drunk. The brothers reluctantly returned home and Wayne closed and bolted iron shutters before he crawled into bed beside Abbie. His gun belt was looped over the bedpost and the rifle lay on the floor. It was a long time before they slept.

Early the next morning, Wayne again cut for sign. Some distance out, on a line with the windows, he picked up an empty cartridge case. He turned the bright copper about in his fingers and looked at the house. Here the killer had made his try. In another moment he found the second cartridge case. There was nothing else.

He showed the cases to Abbie who thought they might identify the killer, but Wayne knew half the men in Arizona had rifles that would use this kind of shell. He pocketed the cases and had breakfast, a silent and thoughtful meal.

He pushed back his chair and reached for his hat. "Abbie, stay inside and don't show yourself. I'm going to bring Hank Malloy out here."

He rode to town and on a hunch went to the

Gila and found the marshal at the bar, talking to Ewing Vance while Inez listened from the far doorway. Wayne told Hank what had happened.

The marshal swore under his breath. "It sounds like you sure as hell got an enemy."

"None that I know of. I'd like for you to look around. Maybe you can cut sign that we missed."

Hank hitched at his gun belt, finished his drink. "Sure."

Ewing Vance picked up the marshal's empty glass, dunked it in the water pail under the bar. He regarded the swinging batwings. There was a stir and he looked around. Inez stood a few feet away.

Her beautiful eyes were knowing, accusing, her voice flat and expressionless. "You missed."

"I missed—twice." He carefully polished the glass and looked at the batwings. "I'll have to leave Nelson alone for a while. But—" He held the glass to the light. "But there are others—seven others."

Down the street, in the freight station office, Canby Tryon worked over the ledgers. On quiet Sunday mornings the big building was not abustle with men loading wagons, cursing at stubborn teams, breaking in with a hundred interruptions. The street was empty, except for an occasional stroller. Glancing out the window, he saw Wayne Nelson go into the Gila. He heard a thud of a heavy crate in the big room beyond the office and

Canby turned back to the ledge. His eyes saw the figures, but they didn't have meaning to a brain busy with the problem of Lew Kearney out there in the warehouse.

He heard slight stirrings and each small sound distracted him. Finally he closed the ledger and heaved up from the desk. He walked out to the warehouse, a fat little gamecock with an oversize military mustache.

Lew Kearney stacked boxes in neat piles near the loading docks. Canby watched him in silence, noting the even features, reluctantly admitting that Lew was handsome enough to catch any girl's eye. A good, steady worker, too—he caught himself, cleared his throat. "Lew!"

The man straightened and he looked gigantic in the half light. Canby bristled as he was forced to look up into Lew's questioning face. "You're doing a lot of extra work."

Lew wiped sweat from his cheek. "Tomorrow's a big day. If I get my load ready now, I can pull out sooner in the morning."

Canby's shrewd eyes challenged and disbelieved. Lew's smile weakened. Canby sucked in his lips. "You're wasting your time. I'm no fool, young man. You're setting your cap for Lorain. I've seen her watching you. I'm aware that she has taken to coming here on Sundays while you're putting in extra work—for no pay. You're wasting your time. My daughter, sir, is not to be married to someone in my hire. She deserves more than a common teamster."

Lew's fists clenched with his effort to control his voice. "I'm young and I'll go a long way, be worth as much or more than you."

Canby smiled coldly. "That remains to be seen. You forget something else, young man. No damned Rebel will ever marry into the Tryon family."

"By God—!" Lew took a lunging stride toward him.

The little man's jaw thrust out and he drew up, bristling, to face Lew, who caught himself up. Canby glared, then let his shoulders drop. His voice came crisp. "We have things to clear up between us, sir. You can continue to work for me on this basis—or you can quit. Suit yourself."

He re-entered the office, firmly closing the door. He sat down at the desk and opened the ledger again. A moment later, he saw Lew Kearney stride angrily down the street. Canby settled placidly to his work. He had dealt the cards straight, and face up. That was good. Even better, he knew that Lew would not quit—and the boy was a fine worker.

When Wayne and Hank Malloy came to the house, Abbie made the marshal welcome and coffee was waiting. They showed Hank the bullet scars. He bumbled about, squinting at splintered rafter, the cracked bullet hole in the adobe wall, then at the window, open to the morning breeze.

They sat down at the table and Wayne told him what had happened, Abbie adding details. Hank pulled at his mustache and took refuge in his coffee cup. Later, the three of them scouted out where the ambusher had hidden. Hank tried vainly to pick up further sign.

They returned to the house and more coffee. Hank again tugged at his mustache. "This ain't Apache work, Wayne. It's plain enough someone wants to kill you."

"That's ridiculous!" Abbie exclaimed.

Hank held out his hand, palm up. "Then what else is there?"

Wayne protested, "I've had no arguments or fights. There's just no reason!"

Hank sighed and arose, reaching for his hat. "You sure can't argue away those two bullets. You keep your eyes open all the time—wherever you go. From now on, don't go out that door unless your Colt's strapped to your leg."

After he left, Wayne and Abbie looked at one another and Wayne helplessly shrugged. She hugged him tightly and then hastily turned to wash out the coffee cups. That night, the iron shutters were tight closed and bolted and the kitchen was stifling with heat as they cooked and ate.

Word of the mysterious attack spread, and grew in the telling. For a week it held the attention of the whole town and then died down as other gossip took its place. A second week passed. Late one night at the beginning of the third, Inez Vance rolled over in the bed and suddenly snapped awake. Ewing had slipped out. She sat up, trying to pierce the pitch blackness of the room. The night was oppressive, still beyond measure, and the desert pressed in silent threat against the house.

She had experienced this feeling before, as though just beyond the circle of sight pressed black eternity through which Edward must wander. She threw aside the covers and groped for matches.

The match was a feeble flicker and then the lamp's reassuring glow filled the room. A voluminous gown covered her but her full breasts rounded the fabric. Her hair, loose now, fell in soft black ringlets. She moved into the living room. Ewing was not there. The house was empty. She walked down the short, narrow hall to the kitchen.

She stopped when she heard the outer kitchen door rattle softly. It swung open and she clutched her gown at the throat. The distant glow of the bedroom lamp faintly touched the door.

Ewing slipped in. Her eyes fastened on the heavy knife in the sheath at his belt. Like his Indian warbow and arrows, that knife had been on a closet shelf since they had first come to

Florence. Ewing turned, stopped short in quick alarm. Then relief flooded his face.

"You should be in bed."

"I woke up. You were gone." She pointed. "The knife?"

His hand touched the handle. The lean line of his jaw tightened but his flecked green eyes did not meet hers. She asked, "Who?"

He did not reply and his eyes did not move. She knew that the light behind her must silhouette her legs and body through the cotton gown. He moistened his lips. "Scipio Adams."

His eyes lifted, glittering. "He thought I came as a friend. Treachery for treachery."

Her lips slowly broke into a smile and again his eyes flicked over the black silhouette of her body. She said softly, "Come to bed."

She turned as he took an eager step forward.

VI

The sky was so blue it hurt the eyes. The far distant mountains were hazy, purple and sharp, even with distance. A breeze moved over the bare desert knoll, tousling hair on bared heads, whipping calico skirts or dark bonnet ribbons, whispering sand against the black box that held the body of Scipio Adams.

Wayne Nelson reached for Abbie's hand as the coffin lowered into the hole. He looked beyond to the mound and headboard marking Bedford Drumbo's grave. Down the slope, clear and magnified in the sunlight, stood the town and the sun glinted off the river. The vast sweep of desert, sky, and mountain made everything insignificant and this burial of a kindly man of no moment.

The preacher held his hand over the grave and the coarse earth, trickling between his fingers, made a hollow sound as it struck the box. Wayne's lips flattened. This *was* of moment, this senseless killing. His eyes sought those who had come the long way with Skip. Vic Hayes and Hal Grayson were absent, but the other four stood near.

Frank Burrud looked carved from stone. Joel Ramsey stood nearby, desolate, hat held before his chest, lips pursed. He lifted his head at that moment and Wayne read fear in the china blue eyes. Lew Kearney stood with shoulders rounded, lips pulled in between his teeth. Jesse Burrud, beside Lew, shifted his weight and his fingers tightened on his hat brim, the slight action an echo of Joel's fear.

There stood Hank Malloy, a square monolith against the sky—Ewing Vance, flecked green eyes held spellbound on the open hole—Inez Vance, whose black, white-trimmed dress accented her dark face and brooding eyes. Yet Wayne had the strange feeling that a smile lurked just below the surface.

It was over, at last. As he and Abbie walked away, Lorain Tryon joined them, and Abbie welcomed her with a quick, warm smile. Lorain spoke to Wayne but her eyes sought Lew Kearney. He walked away with the Burruds and Joel, listening to Frank's low talk. Her face fell.

She asked Abbie to visit with her. Wayne set a time to pick Abbie up and went on to the Gila Saloon. It was crowded. Both Vance and Joel, now in bar aprons, tried to fill a stream of orders. Wayne joined the Burruds and Lew Kearney at a table and, a moment later, Joel bustled up.

His eyes caught Frank's. "What are we going to do—?"

"Not now, Joel. Bring us drinks around."

Hank Malloy left the crowd about the bar and,

smoothing his mustache, left the saloon. There was silence as the batwings whispered and the marshal's boots clumped across the porch and were gone. Then a sigh swept the crowd. A voice said loudly, "You'd think he'd be doing something about this killing."

A babble arose, supporting or condemning Hank. Most felt that Skip Adams' murder was the act of a madman and, with this, the talk reached an impasse. A madman—then who? It could be someone apparently living a placid, normal life. It could be anyone—and anyone could be the next victim. The talk died into a horrible wonder as each stole a look at his neighbor.

Ewing Vance broke the silence. "Something has to be done. We don't know who it is and we don't know who'll be next. But I know Hank would do something about it—if he could."

"Can't he?" someone asked.

"Hell! All of you know Hank. He's a good man . . . good to lock up a drunk. But now we're facing a secret killer right here in our town. Given time, Hank might find him but . . . do we have the time? Who's next? . . . And when?"

Silence held the room. A man cleared his throat. "What you figure we ought to do?"

"I don't know. Maybe if we all think about it, we'll get an answer. But, hell! Let's drink up before we scare ourselves to death!"

Lew Kearney hitched closer to the table.

"Frank, maybe Vance *is* right. We ought to think about it."

"We will. Vic's taking the run to Tucson. He'll be back tomorrow. Hal ought to be back the day after. He's horse trading out toward Casa Grande. We'll see then."

Lew eased back, satisfied.

That night, Wayne made doubly sure of the heavy iron shutters and checked the thick, stout bar across the door. He watched Abbie undress by lamplight and he wondered, sickeningly, if she was safe from the knife that murdered Skip Adams. He was fearful of going on the long trip to the mines but Abbie promised she would be careful both night and day.

When he returned, five days later, he was almost sick with relief at the sight of her. They ate supper in the dead, stifling heat of the closed room. They had just finished when there was a jolting knock on the door. Wayne slipped his gun from the holster and pressed his ear against the door while Abbie grabbed up the rifle in the corner near the cupboard. "Who is it?" Wayne asked.

"Joel—Joel Ramsey."

Wayne lifted the bar, held the Colt with its hammer dogged back as he swung the door open. Joel, worry lines on his round face, saw the weapons in their hands and smiled crookedly. "I don't blame you."

"Get in! You make a perfect target for someone out in the dark." Joel hastily jumped inside. "What brings you, Joel?"

"I'm going to the Burruds'. They want you there. It's important. We're going to talk things over and—well, they want you."

Wayne shrugged. "We'd better go, Abbie."

Joel said, embarrassed, "Maybe just—Wayne? He won't be long."

Abbie sensed the situation and she smiled. "Go ahead, Wayne. I've been safe enough for several nights now."

The Burrud house was large, solidly and comfortably built. Jesse admitted them and Wayne stepped into a long room, thick walls broken by narrow windows, a dark, cold fireplace dominating one end. Hal Grayson and Lew Kearney sat on a horsehair sofa. Frank Burrud stood before the fireplace, legs spread, hands clasped behind his back. Vic Hayes stood by a window, face dark with anger. Jesse indicated kitchen chairs. "Rest yourselves. We'll be here a spell."

Wayne looked around at the six men whom he had come to know so well. Jesse sat near the fireplace. Joel's cheerful expression had vanished and Lew avoided Wayne's searching look. Grayson's eyes glittered from some inner turmoil while Vic Hayes was openly angry.

Frank Burrud spoke. "Wayne, I sent Joel over

to get you. You're involved in this business as much as the rest of us. I want you to tell the boys about the shooting at your place."

Wayne repeated the story, all of them listening attentively. When he finished, Frank looked around. "All of you can see the pattern. First Bed was killed and it was made to look like Apaches done it. But now we know better."

Vic Hayes exploded, "That's what I've always said!"

Frank's quiet look silenced him. "Then Wayne was shot at—a drygulch attempt, at night, when no Apache would stir about. Now Skip is murdered. But this time it can't be blamed on raiding Indians."

"It all fits," Grayson snapped.

"It fits." Frank looked slowly about the circle of faces. "There can be no doubt. Nine of us come here together. Nine of us must die . . . two are gone already."

Wayne caught his voice. "But good God!—why! Bed Drumbo and Skip Adams never hurt anyone in this town or made any enemies. I know damn well none of us have."

"That's not the reason."

"Then someone in this town is insane—killing crazy. It can't be anything else."

Frank ran his fingers through his iron gray hair. "There's something you have to know. But you've got to promise to keep it a secret. Tell

Abbie, she ought to know—and to be ready for what comes. You'll *both* keep the secret?"

Wayne nodded. "And I vouch for Abbie."

"There were eight of us when we met you. All of us had served in the Confederate Army, just as we said. But there was something more. All eight of us blindly joined up and served for a short time under Quantrell."

Wayne could not hide his shock. In four years of Civil War there had been many cruel, unjustified and even beastly actions; Andersonville and Libby prisons, the burning and pillaging of the Great Valley of Virginia were some, but there was at least a shadow of justification.

Quantrell had none. He had gathered the killers, rapists and robbers of the Missouri-Kansas border and had used the cover of war to loose these hounds of evil. Both North and South despised and hated him.

The six watched Wayne intently; Grayson and Vic Hayes with something of challenge, Joel Ramsey in a silent plea for understanding, Lew Kearney's eyes slid away.

"Lawrence?" Wayne asked harshly.

A shadow of pain crossed Frank's face. "That doesn't tell it all, Wayne."

"Just about!"

"You don't understand. All of us lived in Missouri. We felt the cause of the South was right and just."

"But Quantrell!"

"Not all Quantrell's four hundred men were cutthroats and robbers. Like us, many joined up with Quantrell in the honest urge to fight for the Confederacy in Kansas and Missouri. Sure, it was to be irregular warfare, but we honestly believed it was to be done for a worthy and noble cause."

"You couldn't help knowing what Quantrell was!"

"You're talking from hindsight, Wayne. At the time he called for volunteers, all of us believed this was our chance to bear arms for our country. We joined up—and that's where all of us first met."

Frank made a hopeless gesture. "We began to see things in the camp we didn't like but we closed our eyes to it, thinking the Cause was enough—and greater. Lawrence taught us different. The looting, the burning, and the murders sickened us."

"But you *were* there."

"We killed no one, burned nothing, stole nothing. Bed Drumbo guarded some prisoners camped in the street. They had just enlisted for a Yank Kansas regiment the night before. The rest of us were here and there about the town. But within half an hour we were hunting one another up. We were sick to our guts and souls of what we had seen. We left the town together and no one noticed our going.

"When we got home, we heard the full story of Lawrence. Quantrell's men were being hunted down like mad dogs. The eight of us were marked to be hung or shot. So we worked our way across the Mississippi and joined the first regular Confederate regiment we found."

Frank stopped. Wayne felt his sincerity and, despite his hatred of Quantrell, Wayne believed him.

Frank sighed. "We hoped by the end of the war the Lawrence business would be forgotten. Then we learned that amnesty would not be extended to the robber bands—and Quantrell's was the worst of the lot. We knew then we couldn't go home. We figured to come out to this country and start a new life where nobody would think we were with Quantrell."

Frank smiled then. "We met you and Abbie. It pleased us when you decided to come on here with us. It made us feel that we could be accepted in the human race again. We could settle here in peace."

"You can. You've paid enough for an honest mistake. I'll say nothing—might not even tell Abbie. If you're going to make a new life here—"

Frank hopelessly threw his hands high. "You *have* to tell Abbie, Wayne. The past has caught up with us. Someone in this town knows we were Quantrell's men."

"But who!"

"We don't know. It has to be someone who was in Lawrence when Quantrell struck. One or more of us has been recognized by someone who figures all of us were raiders—including you."

Wayne stared. "But I was fighting in Virginia!"

"Wayne, the killer believes you were in Lawrence because you came here with us. You're on his list. That's why he tried for you. Sooner or later, if we don't stop him first, he'll get you—like he plans to get everyone of us."

He added grimly, "And two are already dead!"

VII

Wayne came to his feet. “That’s impossible! I’ve done nothing!” Wayne looked around. Their somber eyes returned his stare. “But he can’t believe that—” The enormity of it struck him. “My God!”

Vic Hayes strode to the center of the room, asked harshly, “All right, what are we going to do? We can’t let this son of a bitch kill us off one by one! Do we just go belly-up?”

Frank Burrud answered calmly. “We don’t just give up, Vic. Who do we fight?”

Vic started to make hot protest, then an uncertain look came into his eyes. “There must be something!”

It opened a hot discussion. During it, Wayne gradually faced stark reality. But, still, a portion of his mind refused to believe that he was marked for death. It was too fantastic.

Frank finally summed up the futile discussion. “All we can do is have our rifles and Colts ready. We’ll keep our eyes and ears open for any sign that’ll lead us to this killer. There’s nothing else.”

So the conference ended and Wayne walked out into the desert night with Lew Kearney. Lew matched his long stride, each immersed in his own morose thoughts. Wayne suddenly realized that every black shadow cast by the bright desert moon could conceal a murderer. His step slowed. “What a hell of a thing, Lew. All of us will be jumpy as jackrabbits within a week.”

“Sure, and maybe one of us will be dead.”

Wayne shoved his hands deep in his pockets. “I’m scared, too . . . but more for Abbie. Maybe this killer has her chalked for a bullet. Think he has?”

Lew considered it. “He knows there weren’t any women with Quantrell.”

“Maybe—maybe, but who knows how far he’ll go? This changes things for all of us.”

Suddenly Lew ripped out an oath and then took a deep breath. “Sorry. I’m thinking about Lorain. This sure kills the last chance I ever had with her. If I’m marked for a killing, I can’t let things go on between us. Even if I happen to live but this thing comes out, what chance have I got! It’s bad enough to be a Johnny Reb as far as her Paw’s concerned, but to be known as one of that Quantrell bunch—God damn it!”

He stalked off toward the group of tethered horses. Wayne took a step after him, thought better of it. He knew how Lew felt—all too well. His thoughts were in a turmoil as he walked down the ruts toward his house. He pulled up short just as he was about to cross the bare yard, realizing the moonlight would make a perfect target of him. He grimly reminded himself that from this moment on, a second of carelessness could snuff out his life.

His eyes slowly circled the yard, probing at each shadow. He saw the faint slits of thin light from behind the iron shutters and knew that Abbie waited for him. He crossed the yard in long hurried steps.

Abbie admitted him when he gave the little series of knocks that had always been their signal. He pushed her aside, closed the door and dropped the bar. He turned to find her looking at him, a brow raised.

"Something's wrong—bad wrong." She made it a statement.

He looked at the stove, wanting time, wondering how to tell her. "There's coffee?"

She poured two cups and then sat down across from him. The lamplight made her eyes emerald green. She watched him a moment then touched his hand. "Darling, you're trying not to scare me."

"No," he denied, then grinned sheepishly. "Maybe that's right, and I know better. I'll tell it straight—as I heard it."

She listened. Her eyes widened in horror when Wayne told the true cause of the deaths of Drumbo and Adams, and her fingers came up to her lips. He told her what they might expect, and why, and looked up to see a slight quiver of her lips.

He took a quick drink of the hot coffee to hide a surge of fear and panic that swept over him. He carefully spoke at last. "During the war, lots of snipers shot at me—and missed. Maybe this will be no different. Once you expect one, you have a chance, anyhow."

"You'll not take a step out the door, Wayne, without your belt and gun. You'll wear it everywhere."

She considered steps they could take to protect themselves, trying hard to speak calmly. Her talk was as much for Wayne's benefit as for hers. Her eyes widened with a new thought. "Wayne! This killer thinks you're one of Quantrell's raiders?"

"Sure. Why else am I marked?"

"But, don't you see! If he knew that you fought the whole war in Virginia and Pennsylvania—no further west than Lookout Mountain, he'd leave you alone."

Wayne sighed. "It might work, Abbie, but how do I deny being with Quantrell without telling the whole town that the others rode with that guerrilla?"

"But to save your life—!"

"If folks knew this about them, they'd be hated right out of town. Some might even try to kill them, and one bushwhacker's enough. They saved our lives, Abbie. I can't throw their chances away just to save my own hide."

"I know," she said contritely. She watched him

pace to the stove, the barred door and back to the table. She said, despairingly, "If you could get word, somehow, to the killer alone. That'd keep their secret."

"But we don't know!" He stopped short and snapped his fingers.

She looked up. "Yes?"

"Everyone talks about the War. Why shouldn't I! I could do a little boasting—where I was, where I marched and what battles I fought. I could talk in the freight yard, the stable, the saloon, the store—most any place. People would know then I couldn't possibly have been at Lawrence!"

"Wayne, that's it!"

"The killer, whoever he is, will be bound to hear me in one of those places. He won't say anything, but he'll take me off his list. Anyone else will think I'm just doing windies about the War."

"And it will keep the secret!" She kissed him. "I'll talk, too, wherever I go. Maybe he'll hear me, or some of the ladies will spread the word. Darling! we've got the answer!"

They talked eagerly, perfecting the plan. Then Abbie looked at the clock, started. "Wayne, you've got to get your rest for tomorrow's work!"

They carried the lamp to the bedroom and, still talking, undressed. He blew out the lamp and climbed in beside her. Her arm went up along his chest, her fingers resting on his cheek as she placed her head on his shoulder. "Wayne?"

"Yes."

"If this man knows they're Quantrell's raiders, why hasn't he told everybody? That'd drive them out."

"I'd guess the raiders did something pretty bad to him—or his. He wants to do his own killing."

She shivered in his arms. "Poor Bed and Skip!"

They were silent until Abbie stirred. "If it was something that happened to him, then *he* was at Lawrence. You could ask around—who was in Kansas. Maybe that'll catch him."

"It might."

Wayne stared up in the darkness, feeling the warmth of Abbie's slender body, the swell of her breasts, the curves of her beautiful legs. Panic swept over him—and the cold sweat of fear he had often known just before a battle. He fought it down, the intensity of the mental struggle bringing sweat to his forehead. He didn't want to die! He had too much to live for! Maybe he and Abbie should pack up and get out of here before—

He choked that back. How many times had he wanted to run during that long, bloody struggle in the wilderness and just before Gettysburg? The bitter taste of fear was in his mouth then as it was now, the worm of it lunatic in his brain. Run!

No—there were worse things than running. But Abbie might also be killed!

She sensed his tension and she pulled him close. He felt her tremble. His own fear evaporated in the need to comfort her. Later, emptied and tired emotionally as well, he was drifting off to sleep when he heard a slight scraping, a metallic click on Abbie's side of the bed.

"What's that?"

"The rifle," she answered. "I made sure it's handy."

He smiled and his hand sought hers. He drifted toward sleep. With a courageous woman like her, how could he think of running?

How could he help but win!

VIII

There was little chance to put the plan into immediate operation. A new mine, opening in the Superior region, needed supplies, material, and equipment in a hurry and the job took most of Canby Tryon's freight wagons.

The loading alone left Wayne so weary at the end of the day that he could only eat and fall into bed. But he did talk at the station about the battles in which he had fought. Anyone listening would know that he had never been near Kansas, let alone Lawrence.

When the long string of wagons pulled out, Wayne wore his gunbelt and he placed it under his blanket at night. He noticed that Lew Kearney was equally cautious—and more withdrawn. At least three times on the trip Wayne brought the campfire talk around to the part he had played in the War. This bunch, at least, would never associate him with Lawrence. He hoped fervently that he might have talked to the killer.

They finally returned to the town. As soon as he could, he left Canby's warehouse and hurried home. He didn't realize how tense he had been until Abbie met him at the door, threw her arms about him and led him inside. He told her of the trip and she reported that all had been quiet. She had gossip to relay, including the fact that Lorain Tryon looked as though something badly troubled her. Abbie guessed that there was mounting friction between the girl and her father.

"Nothing more about . . . ?"

"*He* has made no move," she said. "And neither has Hank Malloy! The whole town's mad. Frank Burrud said there's a meeting tomorrow, at the Gila Saloon. He wants you to be there if you came back in town."

Late in the afternoon, he made the short ride to the Burruds'. They made Wayne welcome and, farmer-wise, talked of the weather. Frank wiped sweat from his forehead. "Hot now—what's it going to become full summer!"

"Blasting . . . Learned anything about who killed Skip?"

"Not a thing. We've been checking. The only Northern man is Canby Tryon but he came out here before the War started."

"He's no killer. Everyone else is from the South?"

"No further north than Kentucky. Hal and Vic both say we'll get nowhere. One of us'll go like Skip Adams and we'll be as much in the dark as ever. . . ."

"Then what do they want to do?"

"They say we should go somewhere and start over again. But if we run now, we'll run all the time."

They looked out across the yard toward the river and the shimmering hills beyond. Where would it end? Wayne wondered. And, from the grim look on the faces of the Burrud brothers, he knew that they had the same thought.

Frank broke the silence. "I reckon Abbie's given you word about the meeting. Hank Malloy has done nothing about Skip's murder. Folks are listening when Vic says Bed wasn't killed by Indians. The town's mad—and worried."

"The killer wants just us," Wayne said.

"But no one else knows it. They think most anybody could be killed next. They're getting scared. They asked Vance Ewing if they could use his place. He agreed, since he don't like the idea of a killer running around loose. You'll come?"

Wayne nodded.

The next evening right after supper, the Burruds hailed the house. Wayne made sure Abbie would be safe, and rode into town with the brothers. When they entered the Gila Saloon, men milled and talked and all the tables were occupied. In a far corner, the mayor sat, eyes troubled. One of his companions drove home a point, forefinger tapping on the table top. The mayor shook his head, frowned.

Lew Kearney came up to Wayne. "Got a minute? I need your advice, bad."

"Sure."

Just then Vic Hayes and Hal Grayson came up. Lew gave Wayne a quick shake of the head and wandered off into the crowd. Hayes looked a touch triumphant. "Glad you made it, Wayne. They're beginning to listen to me. Maybe we can flush out this jasper, with the whole town looking for him."

Hank Malloy pushed open the batwings. He stood within the doorway a long moment, head hunched between his broad shoulders. His mustache accented the bulldog, stubborn set of chin and jaw and his eyes probed about the crowd in a silent challenge. He stepped forward, dropping his hands from the top of the batwings. They whispered shut behind him and he walked down an aisle that cleared for him to the bar. There was silence in the room now as Hank leaned on the bar and harshly ordered a drink. Joel hastened to fill his glass.

Hank drank it, turned, and hooked his elbows on the bar. His eyes cast about the room, challenging, angry. The overhead lamp made a glitter of the nickel star on his shirt. He stroked his mustache and his roving eye rested on the group at the far table. "Mayor, you heading up this shindig?"

The mayor jerked as though Hank's thick thumb had jabbed into his ribs. "No, Hank. I doubt if this is legal, but it's only right that folks have their say—particularly about Skip Adams' killing. You might say I'm just listening."

"Hmmmph!" Hank's eyes moved about the crowd again. "Then who *is* the chief of this powwow?"

There was another silence, broken only by the uncertain shuffle of booted feet. Then Vic Hayes said, "Ewing, you let us meet here. It's only right you head it up. Take over."

Vance looked up, flecked eyes startled but alight. No one spoke. He finally nodded, untied his apron and circled the bar to take a place beside Hank. "If that's what you want I'll do the job."

He waited for further objection, then shrugged in final acceptance. "We want to see if there's something we can do about Skip Adams' killing. It's worried all of us. But we need to know what has already happened since then. Hank, are you anywhere near finding that killer?"

Hank glared about as though seeking a single opponent, then his eyes settled on Ewing Vance. His jaw thrust out but his eyes wavered, fixed again . . . challenging. "I'd be a damn poor lawman if I did nothing about it. I can tell you I'm working on it."

"How?" Vance demanded. "We're entitled to know."

Hank sounded a shade less confident. "Now that's a hell of a question to ask! It could be the killer's right here in this room. You want me to tell what I've done and have him cover his trail?"

Heads turned as neighbor glanced at neighbor. Vance bit at his lip. "But are you getting anywhere?"

"I know what I'm doing. Before long, I'll show that gent that neither me nor the town will stand for a sneaking murderer! You can depend on it."

Despite booming voice, something was lacking. Hank glared about as men shifted, looked at one another, confirming suspicion. Frank Burrud spoke up. "Hank, we're worried. No telling who will be killed next. We *have* to ask if you've found any sign leading to the killer or have any idea who he might be."

Hank's jowls flushed and his eyes sparked, but men waited for his reply. Here and there some of them nodded in agreement. "Damn it! I've told you all I'm going to! Do you want me to show my cards to the killer? I'm doing the job in my own way."

"We realize that, Hank. It's just that we want to be sure."

"You *are* sure!" Hank thundered and tapped his badge. "As long as I wear this, you'll have law in this town. But I'll tell what I think's best to be known . . . and to the right people—not to a bunch gathered like this."

He looked about, big hands fisted. For a

moment he had overwhelmed the crowd with his roaring anger. Vic Hayes stepped forward, spoke slowly, softly, but his words carried to the far corners of the room. "Hank, maybe you know something—maybe you don't. Either way, there'd better be a move damn soon. That killer's not going to wait. He'll hit again unless you stop him."

"He wouldn't dare!"

Ewing Vance made a disparaging noise as he stepped between Vic and the marshal. "Face it, Hank. The killer *does* dare. You understand a drunk or trailing a horse thief. This is something else—and you're lost!" His voice lifted, close to triumph. "The killer knows it. He can kill whenever he likes and there's nothing you can do about it."

He wheeled, leaving Hank stunned by this unexpected, savage attack. Ewing had all of their attention. "Hank's all right to break up fights. But this thing is just plain too damn big for him."

"What'll we do?" someone called.

Ewing's jaw set and his face looked unusually pale but his lips moved in a smile. "Why, it's plain enough. Let Hank go right on as he has—but *we* will take care of this killing business. We'll form a committee—"

"Wait a minute!" the mayor thundered and bulled his way through the crowd. "Committee? Vigilante rule! Is that any way to handle law and order—drumhead court and hangman's noose? By God, it won't happen in this town!"

A babble arose. Ewing lifted his arms for attention and faced the mayor. "It's something we don't *want,* Jeff. No one's against Hank, or hates him. It's just that he hasn't done anything. Let him resign so we can elect or appoint someone who can handle this. Otherwise, the killer's free as the wind to strike again." Ewing's voice lowered. "Believe me, he will. You can bet on it."

Hank's angry bellow shattered the fearful silence. The marshal truculently faced the mayor. "Jeff, am I still marshal?"

"That's right, Hank."

Hank faced the crowd, knotted hands on his hips above the heavy gun belt, and the badge gleamed on his shirt as his barrel chest gustily moved. "You heard what the Mayor said . . . I'm marshal. No one's going to form a vigilante gang while I'm here."

Ewing turned on the law man, his voice a contemptuous lash, "So, you're marshal. Then why don't you have sense enough to resign and let a man with brains take over!"

Hank's heavy jaw dropped and his eyes blinked. Blood suddenly left his face and he stood like a man paralyzed by a blow. Then his thick neck seemed to swell. For a heavy man, he moved with lightning speed. His fist slammed in a powerful upswing that would have torn Ewing's head off.

But the man jerked it aside at the last split second and the blow glanced off.

Even so, Ewing struck the bar and slid to the floor, bumping off the brass rail and thudding onto the sawdust. He sat there, jaw hanging and eyes dulled. Hank turned on his heel, stalked to the batwings and out. They swung violently behind him, leaving a stunned and silent roomful of men.

Wayne grabbed Vance's shoulders and shook him. Vance's head wobbled and then he snapped awake, lips pulling back over his teeth. "Let me at him! I'll kill him!"

Wayne forced Vance down with an effort. The mayor restrained Vance. Wayne snapped, "Take it easy! You've done enough. Get your feathers down. Joel, a drink! Pronto!"

He forced Vance to drink and the saloonkeeper recovered some of his balance. His eyes still smoldered as Wayne sharply studied him, then stepped away.

The mayor called for silence. "Seems like we've all lost our heads and that's no time to make decisions. This meeting's not legal, but you got a right to talk things over . . . calm and peaceful, though, and you're far from it now. This meeting's adjourned until you've all cooled off and can think straight. If you have any ideas, bring 'em to me. But don't get any thought of vigilantes!"

He glared around and then stalked off. It broke up the meeting. Some immediately followed, others milled around and then slipped out. A few remained, some silent, some trying to determine what had been gained. A few spoke against Hank, others for him.

Ewing Vance stood behind the bar, rubbing his jaw, now beginning to discolor. His eyes were mean. As Wayne moved up to the bar with Frank Burrud and Lew Kearney, Vance grabbed his apron with a vicious swipe and busied himself serving the few who remained.

Frank soberly considered his drink. "Looks like we didn't get much done tonight—and that little all wrong."

Ewing's voice rang with assurance. "We got one thing done, friend. We made sure of another killing. You watch! We'll have it sure as hell. Get rid of this law man, I say!"

Frank spoke dryly. "Maybe you'd consider the badge?"

Vance stared at him a long moment. "Yes . . . maybe I would. There's things to be done in this town that Hank Malloy can't do."

IX

Vic Hayes broke in, "By God, Frank! I'd far rather bet on Ewing's brains than Hank's."

Vance raised a deprecating hand. "I'm just saying that we've got to cut sign on this killer."

Hayes snapped, "That's reason enough!"

He caught Frank's warning glance and gave his attention to his drink. The talk moved on and Wayne brought it around to the War. He spoke in detail of his exploits as he covertly watched all who listened, needing to drive home in some unknown mind—present, he hoped—that he was innocent of Lawrence.

Vic Hayes and Hal Grayson eased away from the bar and out of the room. Wayne caught Lew Kearney's frowning look in the big bar mirror. Ewing Vance filled Wayne's glass again. "Seems like you were just about everywhere."

"All over Virginia, that's certain."

Vance shrugged. "A man sure gets around in wartime."

The group broke up, Wayne leaving with the Burruds and Lew. They stopped on the edge of the canopied porch, adjusting their eyes to the night, the black sky diamond-studded with stars. Lew Kearney spoke irritably. "Wayne, lately you talk a lot about all those battles you were in."

Frank Burrud stepped down into the dusty street. “Let’s move along.” The others followed, sensing command. A few yards away, he quietly asked, “Lew, don’t you know why?”

“Just talking big . . . but it ain’t like him.”

“Let him talk. He’s saying he was never in Lawrence and he’s also keeping our secret like he promised. Think things out before you talk, Lew. Good night.”

The brothers walked off and the night absorbed them. Lew shifted uncomfortably. “Wayne, I’m a fool.”

Wayne laughed, relieved. “But something else worries you. Let’s talk about it.”

“It’s Lorain. I’m in real trouble.”

“Canby?”

“I wish that was all! Damn this Lawrence business! Is it going to stay with me all my life?”

“It might. What’s happened?”

“She’s afraid of her Paw and what he’ll do if we keep on seeing each other. She finally decided she’d tell him how she felt.”

“Did she?”

“No—I stopped her. Any day, any time, until this killing business is over, I can be bush-whacked. Where would Lorain be then?”

“Have you told her?”

“How can I without hurting the others? Now, she thinks I’ve found someone else. She’s mad.

I don't blame her but I can't explain. What can I do!"

"I don't know, Lew. There's not much you can do now. But maybe we'll find the killer before very long."

"And maybe I'll be dead before very long—or you. A hell of a thing!"

Lew turned on his heel and walked off. Wayne glanced at the lights streaming over the batwings of the Gila and sighed. A hell of a thing, as Lew had said. But maybe tonight, if the killer had listened, Wayne was out of the shadow of death. He wondered how he would know.

The thought remained with him on the short ride home. Abbie opened the door to his peculiar knock and he stepped inside. He told her what had occurred as they undressed for bed. They blew out the lamp and lay side by side in the darkness, the still air pressing on their uncovered bodies, the room pitch black because of the closed shutters.

Abbie said suddenly, "Hank's not very good, is he? But I think the Mayor's right. What would a vigilante committee do if they found the killer?"

"Hang him, I guess."

"Suppose it was the wrong man? What a horrible thing that would be!"

Wayne said nothing. Sweat was a moist blanket about his body. Abbie sought a relatively cool place on the far edge of the bed. Her voice came out of the darkness again. “Who had the idea for the vigilantes?”

“Ewing Vance.”

“I wonder why. . . . Darling, I think I’ll spend a lot more time in town.”

“Why?”

“Gossip. It’s surprising what women can know. I’ll listen to clacking tongues. Maybe I’ll find out someone we don’t even suspect comes from Kansas.”

He chuckled. “You might get somewhere at that!”

“Women always get somewhere. Look where I got with you!”

Back in town, a light glowed in a small house just around the corner from the livery stable. Hal Grayson sat at the table, staring moodily at a nearly empty bottle of whiskey. Vic Hayes, across the table, reached for the bottle and refilled his own glass. His voice was a growl. “What the hell did we get done tonight? We just talked, damn near had a fight—and that’s it.”

Grayson glanced toward the window with the lowered, cracked curtain and pictured what might be lurking out in the night. He hastily pulled his eyes away. “That’s as much as Hank Malloy has done.”

Vic exploded, “Now that’s the truth! You know,

maybe old Frank had a real good idea when he asked Ewing if he'd like to wear the badge. Ewing strikes me as a man who'll do something."

Grayson dismissed it. "The saloon takes his time."

"Sure, but there's his wife and Joel. They could handle the business while Vance wears the badge."

"Maybe you're right. Joel's a good barkeep and his wife . . . Ever really looked at that wife of Ewing's?"

"Who wouldn't! I could sure keep busy with a woman like her."

Grayson thoughtfully knuckled his chin. "It's something else. I've only seen her three-four times, and then through the crack of that door. I get a funny feeling about her, Vic."

"Hell, so do I! Like I said, a good-looking woman . . ."

"Real funny," Grayson cut in. "Like I've seen her before. It keeps coming to my mind and slipping away again. Of course, I've always rambled around and the War took me lots of places. God knows how many people I've seen one time or another—alive and dead, happy and miserable, laughing or scared."

"Maybe that's it." Hayes pushed the bottle to his companion. "Here, finish it up."

Hayes walked to the window and lifted one edge of the shade, peered out. Grayson watched, understanding the man’s nerves. Hayes returned to the table. “What about you and me?”

Grayson shrugged. “I reckon we stick it out with the rest of them.”

Hayes plumped down in his chair. “Hal, are you sure that’s the right thing to do? It’s better to be alive somewhere else than dead here.”

“But, Vic—”

Hayes cut in. “If we had a chance to meet this killer face to face, it’d be different. But a knife in the back, or a bullet through the window! You never see him! You haven’t a chance!”

Grayson somberly considered his friend. “I can’t argue, Vic. But you’ve got a job. I’m beginning to make some horse deals. So running out is throwing everything away. We’ll be broke and on the move again—saddle tramps, as the cowboys call ’em.”

Vic Hayes studied Grayson from under his brows and came to a decision. His voice lowered. “We don’t need to be broke, you and me.”

Grayson laughed. “What the hell else will we be! Everything we’ve got’s on our backs except what we’ve made for ourselves here. Leave it—and we won’t be busted?”

Vic said quietly, “A lot of times the stage carries bullion or mine payrolls. There’s no passengers. It’d be easy—if we want it bad enough.”

Grayson’s jaw dropped. “Vic, do you know what you’re saying?”

"Of course I do! I'm saying we got a chance to get enough money to take us clean out of the country—maybe South America. You and me could live like kings down there, or in Mexico, with what's in just one strongbox on that stage."

Grayson's face paled and he moved his hand aimlessly along the edge of the table. "You're scaring the hell out of me."

"I'm scared of it, too, Hal. But I'm just as scared to stick around here. I wouldn't say anything to the others, but you 'n me are close friends."

"I know," Grayson worriedly agreed. His eyes rested on the empty whiskey bottle. He grabbed it as an exhausted swimmer would a plank. "We need more whiskey. I'll be right back."

He was up and out of the room before Hayes could protest. Alone, Vic wondered about himself. He clasped his hands, the thumbs lifted, and he stared at them, ashamed that he had even thought of the contents of the strongboxes. But fear welled up. Though Vic Hayes would meet any open assault, the thought of an assassin, a lurking, unseen death made him inwardly frantic. He had concealed it so far, but he did not know how much longer he could control his nerves.

To go far enough to be safe took money. The strongboxes carried it . . . And yet . . . ? He slammed his fist on the table, paced back and forth in the boxlike room.

Hal Grayson walked slowly along the darkened street. He was shocked, but still the idea would solve all their problems. Direct action was certainly preferable to supinely awaiting a murderer's convenience. The thought made him move into the shadow of a building and look hastily about. Then, angry at this gnawing fear, he moved on, alert to catch any small, suspicious sound.

Joel and Ewing Vance busied themselves at final chores in the saloon before closing it for the night. Joel looked around in surprise when Vance came in and ordered a bottle of whiskey. Joel asked, "Late, ain't you?"

"Vic's at my place. Drop around when you're through."

Hal walked out, the bottle under his arm. He again clung to the shadows. He stopped once under a dark store canopy and probed the night. Satisfied, he moved on a few yards, stopped short, thinking he heard a secretive sound. Nothing. He softly expelled his breath.

Without warning, a bulky shape materialized out of the shadows. He caught the faint glitter of a gun in the man's hand. His breath sucked in and his throat constricted. The white blur of the face came into focus and he saw the star on Hank Malloy's shirt. The marshal's voice held a note of surprise. "Hal Grayson! Stand hitched."

The sweat popped out over Hal's body. "My God! Scare a man to death!"

"You'd better talk fast and straight. What are you doing?"

"Hank, what the hell do you mean!"

"You've been hugging the shadows, walking catfoot, looking around. Afraid of being seen?"

Hank's rough treatment roiled Grayson. He spoke through set teeth. "Lately, a man has to be careful in this town. There's a killer loose that our marshal can't catch—or hadn't you heard?"

"Grayson, by God—!"

Hal made his tone a raking spur. "I went to the saloon to get a bottle of whiskey. Vic Hayes is at my place and I've invited Joel Ramsey over. You can come along but you're sure as hell not welcome. Now get that damn gun out of my guts or shoot. I'm going home!"

He stormed around the marshal and strode away. Hank's angry shout reached him. "Quit prowling the streets, Grayson! I'm letting you go this time."

Grayson wheeled. "You can't help yourself."

"Don't be so sure. I wouldn't be surprised if you or one of them friends of yours turned out to be the killer. I'm warning you."

Grayson gasped, "One of *us* kill Skip Adams! Why, you thick-skulled, copper-bottomed fool!"

He whipped away, almost running in order to keep from striking the marshal. He was breathing hard by the time he rapped on the door and Vic Hayes opened it. "Hal, I been thinking—"

His words died when he saw Grayson's paper-white, angry face. Hal thudded the bottle on the table, sailed his hat into a corner and looked at Vic, nostrils pinched, a white line about his lips.

He caught his breath and motioned toward the bottle. "Pour the drinks, Vic. We'll be here a while. How do you figure to get that bullion?"

X

The days steadily grew hotter as the year moved toward summer and work became heavier. Canby Tryon's temper increased in direct ratio to the heat and his prosperity. His explosive, meaningless wrath made Wayne consider turning to the farm, his real vocation.

He thought about it as he rode home late one hot afternoon when Canby had been exceptionally irritable and the trapped heat in the warehouse had been almost unbearable. He eyed the Burrud farm as he passed by. The first small fields already yielded vegetables that found a ready market in the town. Wayne rode slowly on, feeling the need to work his own land.

When he rode into his own yard, Abbie eagerly ran out. Wayne dismounted, turned to meet her as she rushed into his arms. She stepped back, sea green eyes drinking him in. "It was a good trip? Nothing happened?"

"A good trip. Nothing happened. All peaceful here?"

"Yes. Lorain Tryon dropped in once for woman talk."

Within the house, Wayne shed his shirt and poured water into a big wooden tub. Abbie began preparations for supper as Wayne bathed. He toweled himself, dressed in the fresh clothing she had laid out. “How is Lorain?”

“Unhappy. She’s certain Lew has found someone else from the way he’s been avoiding her.”

“You didn’t tell her about—Quantrell?”

“Of course not! I told her she was badly mistaken about Lew and that time would work things out. Not that it helped much, poor girl! She’s fair eating her heart out.”

They ate supper and Abbie gave the news of the town. She had seen many of the women, so she was filled with talk of minor events. Wayne listened as he ate. She finished with a sigh. “Darling, there just isn’t anyone in town who was in Kansas during the War.”

“But there has to be!”

“I know . . . but there isn’t. At least no one admits it.”

Wayne frowned darkly at the closed shutters. “Someone’s lying, then—always has. But who?”

“I thought the women would know,” Abbie said ruefully. “I’ve talked to just about everyone. That Inez Vance is a strange one. She’s so beautiful, really. She’s very polite, but you can tell she doesn’t want to be friendly. All the other women talk about it. She keeps them at a distance.”

“Inez Vance,” Wayne said slowly. “Do you reckon she—?”

Abbie smiled resignedly. “No, she and her

husband are from Kentucky. They were married there."

"We can forget them, then."

"She came alive when I talked about the murders," Abbie recalled. "She thinks Hank Malloy is an old fool and he'll never catch the killer before someone else dies at his hands."

"Who else have we got?" Wayne demanded, shoving back his chair as he arose. "Let's sit outside for a while."

"Is it safe?"

"Night's come and we'll have no light in here. Besides, it's cool."

They blew out the lamp and opened the door. Wayne looked out into the moonless, star-studded night. With their chairs in the black shadow along the house wall, they sat gratefully in the faint stir of the night breeze. They talked aimlessly as Wayne looked out across the cactus-studded land that was his. He again felt the urge to work it and asked Abbie what she thought. She was delighted and wanted him to start immediately. "Jesse said just the other day *they* are getting things in shape before the summer heat comes."

"And that's another problem. It'll take a long time to get the first fields ready—maybe deep into summer. I've heard only Indians can work in the sun. They say it'll kill someone who's not used to it."

Abbie said nothing but he sensed her

disappointment. At last he broke the silence. "Maybe you're right."

They were silent again. Wayne made his decision. "I'll freight until fall, quit Canby and take the winter to get ready. That way, we'll have more money and we won't be starting a late crop that the heat could kill."

They lazily made their plans, deciding what section they would break first, what they would plant, forecasting their future in bright colors. Wayne tilted his chair back against the house. He became aware of the drag of the gun belt about his waist, the holster hanging free of the chair. It irritated him but it was as necessary as the rifle he had leaned against the wall. That damned, sneaking killer! He forgot it when Abbie said the Burruds' new irrigation ditch would extend almost to the boundary between the two farms. Wayne might arrange to continue it into his fields.

They looked toward their distant neighbors, seeing only black, star-studded sky. Then they saw an arching streak of light, a pinpoint that lifted over the dark land for a moment, then disappeared.

Abbie exclaimed, "What was that? A shooting star? I've heard that's a sign someone has died."

"Shooting stars generally fall out of the sky. That one lifted up and then fell—sure acted strange."

He tilted his chair back against the house to resume their planning and dreaming. But he froze. He saw a glow near where that puzzling streak of light had fallen. The glow lifted, died, then lifted again, flickering and wavering. "Abbie!"

"I see it. What is it?"

"That's a fire! At the Burrud place. I'm getting over there!"

His chair thudded as he jumped to his feet. He lunged toward the lean-to stable. Abbie's sharp voice halted him. "Wayne! I'm going, too! I might be needed."

"No, Abbie! Can't tell what's happening over there."

"I either go with you or alone, Wayne. If someone's hurt, I can help. If they need another gun, I've got the rifle right here."

She meant it. Impatient though he was, he was proud of her. "I'll hitch the horse to the wagon."

"No time. Saddle up. I'll ride behind you."

Wayne threw the saddle on the horse. In a matter of minutes, he led the animal outside, mounted and reached a hand down to Abbie. She landed behind him with a thud. "Hurry!"

"Hang on."

They raced away. They could see the glow against the sky and suddenly a tongue of flame licked upward. Wayne pulled his gun from the holster and fired twice into the air to signal the

Burruds help was on the way. Abbie clung to his waist, holding onto the rifle. Now they saw the shape of the barn as the flames crowned it with a flickering, devilish light.

They swept into the yard. The barn was a torch of flame and smoke. Frank and Jesse stood silhouetted against the flames as they led a struggling, frightened horse away to safety. The crackling roar of the fire was deafening. Wayne pulled his horse to a sliding halt and Abbie jumped to the ground.

He swung from the saddle, tied the reins tightly around a big post that held a corner of the porch roof. Then he raced across the yard. The brothers now had the horse under control. Frank shouted, "Take him, Jesse." He swung to Wayne. "Thank God you've come! Water buckets—from the well!"

Abbie was already there, the first filled bucket sitting on the well rim. Wayne snatched it up and raced for the barn, hearing the rattle of another empty bucket behind him, then the splash of water.

All of them worked frantically. They formed a scant line; Abbie at the well, then Jesse, Frank, and Wayne. Wayne's breath tore from his chest as he reached for full water buckets, dashed them on the structure. For a time, Wayne thought they would save the barn, but a whole section of the roof exploded in a roaring inferno and they knew it was hopeless. Exhausted, sweating, gasping for breath, they retreated across the yard to the house to watch the flames devour the barn. Firelight played on their weary, drawn faces as they sat on the edge of the porch.

Frank said, "At least all of the stock was out—we saved that much."

They watched the structure collapse with a hissing roar and a shower of sparks. It flamed high, then slowly died as the fire voraciously consumed itself. At last there was no more than a wide area of glowing embers with here and there a wicked lick of small flames.

Jesse spoke in quiet awe. "I never saw anything go so fast!"

"Jesse happened to look out the window," Frank said wearily, "just as the whole thing busted loose. Can't figure what caused it."

Wayne then described the strange streak and their momentary belief it was a shooting star. Frank sharply questioned him. Where had they first seen the streak? What had been its trajectory? Wayne answered as well as he could. Frank looked at the pile of ashes that had been the barn. "This was deliberately set."

Wayne demanded, "You mean someone slipped up and set fire to it?"

Frank made a sweeping gesture toward the outer darkness. "That streak you saw, Wayne. It was a fire arrow."

Abbie exclaimed, “You mean Apaches set this?”

“I don’t think so. It’s an Indian trick but Apaches lay low at night.”

“But why?”

“It’s part of the pattern—against the nine of us.”

Wayne looked toward the outer darkness. When the fire had been at its height, they had been bathed as though by a searchlight. “You’re wrong, Frank. If it had been the killer, we’d all be dead now. We make perfect targets.”

Abbie objected. “But there are four of us. Maybe that’s more than the killer bargained for. One or two would be different, but he ran too great a risk with four.”

“That’s it,” Frank said. “If he killed one with the first shot, he’d know the rest would jump for cover. He’d have three guns hunting him. He didn’t dare take the chance. We’ll look for sign come daylight. I bet we find it.”

Even though they were certain the killer had fled, they did not linger long outside. Wayne helped picket the livestock before he and Abbie started home. Then he rode alert for the sound or sight of danger, but nothing broke the quiet peace of the night. He urged the horse to a fast pace, half expecting to see his own home destroyed when he returned.

But it stood, solid and comforting, when they came into the yard. They dismounted and Abbie helped him unsaddle and stable the horses. They cut hurriedly across the yard to the house. A step or so away from the door, Wayne saw the white thing upon it. He stepped close, saw that it was a ragged bit of paper affixed to the door by a long, sharp splinter.

Abbie breathed, “What is it?”

“Get inside,” he said harshly. “We’ll see.”

They bolted the door behind them and Abbie lit the lamp. Wayne stepped to the table. The paper was a bit of crude, ruled pencil tablet, such as could be found in every house and store in the area. Wayne smoothed it out on the table. They both stared down at the crudely, boldly blocked single word—

LIAR

Abbie’s fingers tightened around Wayne’s arm, her face pale, eyes rounded. “Wayne! The fire! The killer wanted to draw us over there so he could leave this. He’s heard you talking about the War and where you were . . .Wayne, somewhere, sometime, you’ve talked to the murderer!”

He crushed the paper, his face granite. “Yes—and he doesn’t believe me. I’m—still marked, Abbie.”

XI

Morning came, so clear that the hills across the river looked close and sharply etched against the sky. Apparently, here was peace; the easy, slow life of the desert with its rhythm of eternity. The illusion vanished when Wayne looked toward the Burrud place. What had lurked out there last night among the tall sentinel cactus and clumps of desert brush?

Despite Abbie's protests, he circled out around the house looking for sign while she fixed breakfast. He found nothing and, later, he and Abbie hitched up the wagon and drove over to the Burruds'. The ashes and charred remnants of the barn looked repellent in the bright sunshine. Frank and Jesse welcomed them and Wayne told of the note he had found on his door.

Frank gravely shook his head. "He's getting bolder. It won't be long before he'll hit again."

"And all we can do is wait . . . I looked for sign but couldn't find any."

Frank said, "You saw the fire arrow last night. Can you figure from what direction it came?"

They scouted away from the barn in the line of the arrow flight. They walked carefully, separated from each other by several yards. They moved further and further out until Jesse called. He pointed to smudged tracks in the sandy ground. Frank turned to face the farmyard. It was some distance away but the roof of the house could be plainly seen. So would the barn, had it been standing.

Frank said thoughtfully, "He drifted up here from the river. You can see where he came in and then went back."

Wayne judged the distance. "He shot an arrow from here? Seems like a long way out."

"Probably a heavy war bow—and it took considerable muscle to pull it. He arched it high to hit the barn roof. That's why you glimpsed it sailing up over the saguaro. He waited out here in the darkness until me 'n Jesse come running out. There would have been two more dead if you hadn't fired that signal, Wayne."

"No, Frank. He didn't aim to kill—yet. He wanted to get that note to me without a chance of being seen. He figured we'd see the fire from our place and come helling over to help. That gave him the chance."

Frank made no direct comment but indicated the tracks. "Let's see if we can follow them."

Down near the river, Jesse pointed to the clear imprint of a shod horse. They found only one other trace, another partial print of the horse towards Wayne's farm. There was nothing else so they returned to the house.

Frank said flatly, "I'm telling Hank Malloy about this and I want you and Jesse to bear me out. If the law don't do something, we'll all be dead."

Wayne helped Abbie into the wagon and then pulled his hat brim low against the sun. "Abbie, you go home."

She leaned down and placed her hand on his shoulder. "Just be careful!"

They rode into town, a grim trio. They went directly to the marshal's office and Hank glowered up at them as he cleaned a gun at his desk. "What's on your minds?"

Frank dropped unasked into a chair while Wayne and Jesse pulled up two more and sat down. Hank looked suspiciously at each in turn. He read the grim set of their faces and he pushed the gun parts aside. "Is someone else—murdered?"

Wayne snapped, "No, but might have been."

Frank cut in before Wayne could say more. "It happened this way, Hank."

Hank listened. His face tightened and the lines about square jaw and chin deepened. When Frank mentioned their belief that the barn had been set with a fire arrow, he exploded, "That's loco! Only Indians'd use that trick!"

Frank's eyes met his and locked. Hank's jaw suffused an angry red, then his eyes dropped and he impatiently swiped his hand along his mustache. “All right, but I got to see for myself. Maybe we can pick up more sign.”

Wayne did not return with them but went to the freight station. Word of the burning spread over town as though carried on the wind. At the noon rest period, Wayne was surprised when Canby Tryon asked him directly about the incident. Wayne confirmed the destruction of the barn, omitting the rest.

Canby bristled. “This town’s not safe anymore. Two murders and now a burning! Why, they might even burn this place for all we know. Something has to be done—quick and sudden. What has Hank Malloy done! He’s getting too old and too dumb to handle the law badge any more. Lots of others are thinking that way, too.”

Canby stomped off and the talk buzzed eagerly until the men went back to work. Not long after, Wayne saw Hank Malloy ride by. There was something morose in the set of his face; stubborn, challenging, and yet defeated in the way he held his shoulders.

Just at quitting time, Abbie drove up to the station in the wagon. Wayne climbed wearily in the seat and Abbie rein-slapped the horse into motion. They were at the edge of town before she spoke. “Frank says there’s a meeting at his place tonight. You’re to come.”

“And you,” Wayne added. “You’re in this as much as the rest of us. You’ll go.”

She nodded. "Everyone knows what's happened. Hank Malloy went direct to his office and he hasn't come out since. Won't see anybody, I hear."

"Trying to figure it out, maybe," Wayne said charitably.

After supper, they drove to the Burruds'. Frank explained that Joel could not get away from his duties at the Gila Saloon. He spoke to the group with grave deliberation. "I called you in because I believe we'll get no protection from the law. Hank Malloy is as badly lost as a child in the woods. He knows we have him pegged, and so has the town."

"So what do we do?" Vic Hayes demanded.

"I'm not sure. But, first, you'd better know exactly what happened last night."

He told them, calling on Wayne and Abbie to add what they had seen. When he finished, there was a long silence. Frank himself broke it. "We know a fire arrow was used. So someone around here owns an Indian bow—might be from any tribe, east or west. I told Hank this and I showed him what sign we had found."

Grayson asked, "What'd he say?"

"He said he'd ask around." Frank's eyes flashed. "Ask around! As if the killer'd admit having a bow that'd put a hangrope around his neck! Hank should search—tear the town upside down, if he has to!"

Vic Hayes laughed, mocking and scathing. “Wait!—be patient!—let the law handle this! Stick around and fight it out! Remember what you said, Frank? Now what do you think? Should we stick around until we’re burned out or killed off one by one? Can Hank Malloy stop that any more ’n he could stop Bed and Skip’s murders—or this burning! Or the bushwhack on Wayne!”

Frank held out his hands. “What does running gain?”

“Our lives!”

“We’ve risked those before,” Frank said soberly. “The old argument still stands. We’ve started to build something here and we can’t throw it away. We have a chance to get this killer. Only *he* knows about Quantrell but he doesn’t dare tell, for that’ll give him dead away. But we will give ourselves away if we run. It’s not only that other people will figure we’re cowards—but *we’ll know* it—each of us. If that’s what you want, Vic, there’s nothing holding you.”

Hal Grayson gave Vic a swift warning sign and Vic sank back, angry and frustrated. There was a strained silence until Frank asked for suggestions. The meeting finally broke up with little accomplished. Wayne drove home in morose silence.

Abbie finally said, “I guess we all whistle in the dark. What can any of us do? The killer will strike when he’s certain sure and not before.

He'll catch each one alone. What good will the others do them?"

The next morning Wayne entered the warehouse and immediately started to check his load. Canby Tryon appeared in the yard and waved all the men toward him. They formed a curious half circle and the pudgy man glared around at them. "Are all of you citizens of this town? . . . Then we won't roll the wagons until later."

Wayne asked, "What's up?"

"Important meeting. The Town Council's talking with the mayor and folks are gathering at the Gila. The town's upset. The citizens want to know what the mayor and council aim to do."

"Who told the mayor?"

"I did, Nelson. I told him we'd all be waiting at the Gila after the meeting. Now git over there. I want the council to know everyone's back of this."

Wayne and Lew Kearney led the teamsters as they pushed into the Gila. Wayne realized that the greater part of the male population of the town was here. He glimpsed the Burruds in a far corner, then saw Vic Hayes and Hal Grayson in earnest conversation at another table. Voices rose in a low hum.

The bar was lined except for a space toward the very end where Hank Malloy stood alone. He stared glumly at a glass and bottle before him. Wayne hesitated a second and then pushed into the empty space beside the man. Hank's red-rimmed eyes met Wayne's and his lips curled faintly under his mustache.

"Ain't you afraid you'll catch something?"

"No."

Wayne signaled Joel Ramsey. Hank returned to contemplation of his drink. His fingers curled around the glass then suddenly he tossed down the whiskey and poured the glass full again.

Wayne accepted his drink and Joel hurried on to other customers. Ewing Vance worked hard and fast. Wayne listened to the talk. The conversation was low, for none as yet wanted to speak openly in front of Hank. But the law man listened. Wayne studied the heavy face in the bar mirror, saw the gleam in the murky eyes, the big hand tighten about the glass, relax again. Hank tossed off two drinks as Wayne nursed one along.

This murmuring would get nowhere until definite word came from the town officials. Each time the batwings swung open, there came a momentary lull in the talk. It broke out again when the newcomer was seen to be of no importance.

Hank poured yet another drink and stared at it as though he read his future in its amber depths. He swiped the back of his hand across his nose and mustache and shook his head like a wounded bear.

The man to Wayne's right spoke none too softly

of the need for a "real law man in these parts." He repeated the stories Wayne had heard, twisted slightly. Wayne glanced at the mirror. The law man still stood, head lowered so that his hat brim hid his face. His fingers worked at the star on his shirt. He unpinned it, placed it beside the glass and stared at the glittering nickel for a long time. He suddenly straightened, rapped loudly on the bar and his heavy voice brought everyone about to face him.

Hank leaned back against the bar. His head hung forward, hunched between powerful shoulders. His bloodshot eyes moved over the room, questing among all these hostile faces, challenging each, contemptuous of each.

He groped behind him until his fingers touched the badge and he held it up. "Look at this badge, you bunch of yappin' hound dogs! See it? You pinned it on me, remember? You elected me!"

Wayne heard the whisper of shuffling feet, nothing else. Hank slowly swept them all with his hate-filled look. "I know you're saying I can't handle things no more. You figure I ain't got the brains to catch the snake who did these killings."

He lifted the badge again. "I know what the mayor and council is doing as well as you. I ain't never been fired from a law job—never! I don't aim to be fired now. I've done what I could, but you figure it ain't enough. You ain't willing to wait. So—" He dropped the badge with a ringing clatter on the bar. "Be damned to you, each and every one! Get yourself a new marshal."

In a dead silence he set his hat at an angle, shifted his gun belt and glared around again. He walked straight ahead and men hastily pushed back so a lane appeared before him. He threaded it, boots thumping loudly in the dead silence. His big hands slapped against the batwings and they burst outward. They swung behind him, whispering, empty.

The silence held. The abandoned star lay on the bar, bright against the dark wood. The tension broke as a man far back in the room cursed in awed amazement. Instantly, everyone spoke at once. Some went to the door, stepped outside. They returned to say that Hank had walked toward his house, not his office.

Someone yelled, "Here comes the mayor!"

The mayor pushed through the batwings and stood blinking against the darkness for a moment. Then he stepped into the room, looked around. Ewing Vance hurried up. "Looking for Hank? He just quit. Left his badge on the bar."

The mayor saw the badge beside the whiskey bottle and empty glass. Wayne caught his passing expression of sympathy and understanding. The mayor walked to the bar, reached for the badge, hesitated, then picked it up. He looked at Vance. "So Hank quit?"

"We all heard him. You're holding the badge."

The mayor sighed. "The council voted to fire Hank and get someone else. But it's easier this way."

Wayne caught his voice. "Who did they hire?"

The mayor looked at Ewing Vance. "Can your wife and Ramsey run the Gila?"

"Why . . . I reckon."

The mayor weighed the badge in his hand, sharply studying Vance. "Then you'll wear the badge, Ewing. You've got a chance to back some of your strong talk." He pinned the badge on Ewing's shirt. "You're marshal now—on trial. We want to see what you can do."

Ewing's hand slowly lifted to the metal, touched it. His face lighted, thin lips drawing back in a tight smile. "Mayor, it's—an honor and a duty."

He looked down at the badge, hands fumbling for his apron strings. He jerked the stained cloth from around his waist and pitched it over the bar to Joel. "I accept. I'll do my best to—"

He broke off and Wayne detected a crowing note in his voice. "Mayor, you'll see some action now!"

His face swept the crowd and Wayne was startled for the second Vance's eyes rested on him. They were cold and wicked, glittering with something that sent a tingle along Wayne's nerves. Vance lifted both arms high over his head. “My last act as bartender at the Gala, boys! Drinks are on the house!”

In the stampede to the bar, Wayne was pressed against it. A full whiskey glass appeared before him. Eager voices yelled congratulations and someone stridently proposed a toast. Ewing Vance, flushed and happy, lifted his hands in acknowledgment. The star glittered on his white shirt.

A worm of unreasonable doubt gnawed at Wayne. He derided himself. Ewing Vance had brains. People had confidence in him.

Wayne’s voice lifted with the rest. “To Marshal Vance!”

XII

As soon as Canby Tryon saluted the new marshal with a single drink, he moved through the crowd rounding up his men. Canby impatiently hurried them to the job of hitching the teams and waved each heavily loaded wagon out the wide gates and down the street.

Wayne and Lew were part of a small group driving northward. Many miles along, most of these wagons would strike for Phoenix while Wayne and Lew would head northeast to the mines in that area.

As the hours passed with the steady, rumbling roll of the wagons, Wayne had time to consider what had happened at the Gila Saloon. He felt deep sympathy for Hank Malloy. What did a man do when he learned people no longer trusted him? Hang onto the job? Or quit, as Hank had done? Wayne hoped he would never have to make a like decision.

They took their nooning. Free now of the narrow wagon seats and the constant rumble, the drivers spoke of the Gila and there was little sympathy for Hank Malloy. The town was well rid of him. Wayne listened, taking little part in the comments.

The next morning, Wayne and Lew wheeled

their wagons eastward, splitting off from the others. The hours passed. At the nooning, they lolled in the shadow of the wagons. Lew spoke of what had happened at the Gila Saloon. "Kind of funny to think of Vance as a law man. But he's got a lot of git-up where Hank has sort of let things drift along."

"What have *we* done?"

"Why, everyone of us has kept his eyes open! We've tried to find out who might've been at Lawrence and so wants our hides."

"And we got just as far as Hank—no further. We at least know the killer has some connection with Lawrence. Hank didn't even know that."

"I know—but we couldn't tell him. But, Wayne, he didn't do anything. Maybe Ewing will. There ain't many people in Florence. You'd think there'd be some sort of sign. If there is, Ewing will find it."

"Maybe. I sure hope he does."

"I'll bet on it," Lew said shortly.

"But don't take odds. Vance might have more real brains than Hank, but so has this killer. We can't tell Ewing any more 'n we could Hank."

They camped that night deep in the folds of the barren mountains and were up at the first streak of dawn. Late the next afternoon, they came to a small mining village tucked in the canyons and Wayne pulled in behind the general store. Lew drove on, heading for another mining settlement many miles northeast. It was dusk by the time Wayne unloaded his cargo and tooled the empty wagon to the local livery stable.

The next morning, he started the long ride home. He jolted along the mountain road, eyes squinted against the beat of the sun in the rocky canyons. His mind hop-skipped over the many things that had happened since eight men had rescued Abbie and him from outlaw rifles. He pictured the people he knew in Florence, calling each face up to the mirror of memory, checking over the little he knew of each.

How little! When his life might depend on it, or the lives of his friends. Two of them gone now—and who would be next? Then Wayne thought of Ewing Vance. Why did Vance want the law star so badly? Or had it been pinned on him because he had complained of Hank so loudly? Wayne remembered Ewing's honest surprise when the mayor gave him the badge.

But he had accepted. Why? Wayne grunted irritably and cast the thoughts aside. But they trooped back by the time he made his lonely camp that night. They were with him when he drifted off to sleep, even though he had found many logical answers. Ewing Vance wore the badge. Give the man a chance!

The next morning Wayne had no more uncertainty on the subject. He was soon on the road but taking his time, hoping Lew would catch up with him. The boy would be on his way home, too, somewhere on the back trail.

The long, hot day passed and again Wayne made a lonely camp. Now he had come out of the mountains and headed south toward the Gila River. Ahead of him loomed a low range of hills. Wayne sat humped on the seat, shoulders and hat pulled against the beat of the sun. He moved to stretch cramped muscles and looked back along the road. It was empty. He settled to the seat again.

The road found a way through the hills that silently enfolded Wayne as the wagon rolled on. A hot wind stirred in the defile, forming a dust devil that danced like a whirling dervish right at the wagon, swept over it with a faint rattle. Dust sifted into Wayne's nose and he sneezed violently, jerking forward.

The bullet ripped across his shirt, sending a stinging line of fire along his shoulder, then whined off into the bright sky. The flat report of the rifle made a smacking sound. Indians! flashed through his mind. Apaches wanting horses and a scalp. Wayne yelled at the horses and whacked the reins across their rumps.

He heard a sharp, flat crack again and one of the horses pitched forward on rubbery legs, dead before it hit the ground. The other tangled with it, went down and the wagon slewed around. Wayne dropped over the side even as a third bullet sought him out. He jumped for the horse struggling to get up, pulled the knife from the sheath at his belt and slashed at the tangle of harness.

The horse came to its feet, stood quivering. Another bullet cut a deep scar along the front of the wagon, whined off into space. Wayne jumped to the shelter of the wagon, replacing the knife and snatching his Colt from its holster.

The bullets came from but one direction and Wayne knew his assailant was alone. The killer! he thought grimly, striking when he is sure and certain. He could hear Abbie's words again.

That chance dust devil and sneeze saved him, but the unknown in the rocks still held most of the cards. A Colt wasn't much good against a rifle in this deathly game of ambush and Wayne thought of the Winchester snugged under the wagon seat. He had to get it.

The rifle crashed again and the slug tore into the wooden bed. A second shot came, spaced a little nearer. The killer methodically, though blindly, sought him out, pinned him down. Wayne dropped to the ground near the front wheel as lead smashed through the wagon's side. The horse kicked and snorted and Wayne feared the animal would try to bolt again as the wagon rocked and jerked. But the horse stood, eyes rolling, still partially tangled in harness and held by the traces.

Wayne came to a crouch and looked up toward

the corner of the wagon, placing the seat and the exact location of the rifle. He had but a split second in which to work. He jumped upward, foot braced against the heavy wheel hub. He lined against the sky and felt as though his head and shoulders were as huge as the hills. His frantic fingers touched the rifle, jerked it from the scabbard. He dropped as a bullet split the air where his body had been a second before.

He leaned against the wagon, gaining confidence from the feel of the rifle. He forced himself to breathe deeply and evenly as he cast around for some way out of this trap. He pushed his mind away from fear into a cold survey of his position.

Saguaro—no help. Bare slope at this end of the wagon for a distance of a hundred yards where a cluster of rocks mocked him with an offer of protection. His eyes moved on to the far end of the wagon, saw a smaller cluster of rocks perhaps fifteen yards away. He might be able to make them in a swift dash. They'd give him a chance to see the opposite rim and pinpoint the bushwhacker.

He edged along the wagon. The silence was broken again by the crack of the rifle and Wayne saw dust spurt between the wagon and the rocks. It spurted again as the bushwhacker methodically spaced bullets in a line from wagon to rocks.

Silence again. The bullets had warned Wayne

not to try it. The ambusher had seen this one chance to escape and had covered it. He need only wait now. Time passed. Ten minutes later, a single rifle shot spurted dust below the wagon, warning Wayne that death still waited.

Wayne felt helpless and a futile anger gagged him. He couldn't leave the wagon shelter. But the high bed prevented him from locating the bushwhacker, stopped any slim chance he might have of returning the fire. He couldn't dash for these mocking rocks—the killer blocked him. Pinned—a sitting duck! Tallied as the third of the nine to go!

The unknown was Bed Drumbo's murderer, the man who had killed Skip Adams. Wayne thought of the remaining horse as it moved impatiently, and he glanced at the sun. So he was pinned down—but that would last only as long as the day. Once darkness came, Wayne would cut the animal loose, mount and slip away. If he could cut between the killer and the town, he had a chance of unmasking the man.

He smiled tightly. Then he heard the crack of the rifle again, the ambusher's notice that he still waited to play his cold deck. Wayne laughed sardonically. Not quite as cold as he thought. Wait—just wait!

The rifle cracked again and the horse screamed. Wayne wheeled around in time to see the animal fall, kick convulsively and then lay still.

Silence . . . and despair. No chance, even with darkness. Wayne's breath caught in his throat. The unknown killer had been able to read his mind, it seemed.

He had only to wait up there in the rocks, or move freely to get Wayne in his rifle sights. This was truly a cold deck now.

XIII

There can be silence and yet a man can detect the essence of sound. He can feel movement and every nerve transmits the vibrations of violence. There was only the great, brooding silence of the desert. There was no movement in the limited area of Wayne's vision but he felt that, beyond the high wooden barrier of the wagon, something moved and slithered, evil and violent death were focalized in this sun-beaten canyon.

The steady pressure of heat and sweat made a moist, greasy film on his face. He thought of the canteens under the seat—jerked his mind away. Wayne stood with his back to the wagon, bracing against the high wheel. Time passed. There were no more shots, nothing moved. Wayne dashed the sweat from his eyes and considered the shade under the wagon bed.

He eased down under the wheel and it seemed, in the deep silence, that the sound of his movement could be heard the full length of the canyon. He expected an instant response from the ambusher. But nothing happened. Keeping well away from the far side of the wagon, he gave himself a short period of sheer enjoyment of shade. Cramped muscles eased and a certain amount of confidence returned.

But it was gradually worn away by the slow passing of time. He watched, waited—hopeful that someone would come along or that the ambusher had left, again knowing with despair that he was trapped and it was but a matter of time before he died here.

The sun moved toward the west and the heat and silence became oppressive. He tried to keep patient but at last he could stand the trapped, helpless feeling no longer. He pulled off his boot, jammed the rifle stock in it and slowly pushed it toward the far end of the wagon. From a distance it would look as though he had unwittingly exposed his leg.

The boot slowly extended out into the edge of sunlight. He waited. He moved the boot as a man would shift position of his leg . . . nothing. He pulled rifle and boot back and tried again by the near wheel . . . nothing. He considered the meaning of the continued silence. The killer gone? Too smart for the trick?

He pulled in the rifle and worked his foot into the boot. Impatience and the need for action rode him hard. He eased to the end of the wagon, searching the bare, broken line of hills. He slowly came out, at a crouch, ready to fire at the first object that showed against sky or rocks. He stepped clear, Colt in his hand, hammer dogged back.

There was no smack of a rifle, no sudden flurry

broke the rim line against the sky. Wayne moved slowly, eyes casting ceaselessly about, muscles tensed. He could now see, in the far side of the wagon, the splintered holes where the bullets had struck. He scanned the far canyon wall and marked an upward path.

He started the ascent, slowly at first, and then faster as he became convinced the rifleman had fled. Still, it was some time before he stood on the rim and looked about. It was a barren, level ridge dividing the main canyon from a secondary one. He looked around at empty cartridge cases where the bushwhacker had lain prone and tried to kill him. There were plain marks showing the direction the killer had come, and had gone. Wayne cautiously followed them across the ridge to the gentle slope down into the far, narrow canyon. Droppings showed where a horse had been ground-hitched and Wayne's eyes bleakly followed the marks down the canyon, out of sight around a curve.

No use to follow. He returned to the main canyon rim and looked down on the wagon, then in both directions along the empty road. There were many hot, torturing miles ahead to Florence. Maybe the killer had decided to leave him to the slower, torturing death of the desert.

Wayne descended to the canyon floor and the wagon. He swung upon the seat, pulled the canteens from beneath it. One full, the other nearly so. He rolled up his few supplies in his blanket, roped it into a tight pack and swung it over his shoulder. He looked up at the rim where the ambusher had lurked. The unknown had lost this bullet gamble and now bet on the desert.

"We'll see. By God, we'll see!"

He fit the pack to his shoulder. He knew the desert must be met at its own tempo if he hoped to survive, so he moved with a steady, easy stride. The heat was like a blanket. He trudged on, a pitiful moving speck in an infinity of barren land bounded by distant purple mountains. He clung to one slight hope—someone might come along.

Nightfall found him but few miles along the way. The sun dropped behind the mountains and the short twilight of the desert was on him. He heard the stirring of the crawling denizens who moved, hunted, and killed during the dark night hours.

He found a place near the road and built a small fire of desert brush. In the starlit dark, the flickering fire made a clear pinpoint of light. Wayne sat back from it, still playing safe though he felt certain the killer was many miles away. He wondered why the man had abandoned the bushwhack. He had but one unsatisfactory answer. The man had not wanted to take the chance, once darkness came, that Wayne might slip up on him and the killer would let himself be known.

Wayne's thoughts drifted on. The second attempt on his life had failed. He had been luckier than Drumbo or Skip Adams or the Burruds, who had lost by fire . . . His thoughts froze on that picture.

Abbie alone on the ranch! The killer had failed here, was he now planning an attack on the ranch house? A shiver passed over Wayne and dread seized him. He looked southward as though, even at this distance, he would see a glow against the sky. He could see all too vividly another fire arrow striking his house or a dark figure at the door. What could Abbie do against a death that struck without warning?

A slight breeze stirred and the little camp-fire flames leaped higher, a symbol of what might be happening in town. He hastily rolled up the pack, slung it over his shoulder, picked up the canteens and rifle and strode off. The pinpoint of the fire grew smaller and smaller behind him.

It was much cooler now and Wayne hit a long stride. Yet he was nearly crawling with weariness when the first streaks of false dawn touched the horizon. He dropped beside the road until some measure of strength came back. Then he built another small fire and made a meager breakfast. The eastern sky was bright by the time he finished and he could already feel the promise of heat.

He looked northward, thinking of Lew Kearney or any other early traveler. Nothing. He faced south, the way he must travel. He saw a faint lift of dust—a rider! He thought of the ambusher and slipped behind a tall, thick saguaro. He held his Colt ready. Soon Wayne heard the creak of saddle leather and then the rider appeared.

Wayne first saw the glittering star on a dark shirt, a glint of cartridges in a gun belt. Then he saw Ewing Vance's pale features. The law man rode at an easy slouch, his lips puckered in a soundless whistle. Wayne stepped from behind the saguaro. "Vance!"

The law man's head swiveled toward Wayne as his right hand dropped to his holster. Wayne strode toward him, a wide smile cracking his stubbled, dust-streaked face. "Vance! God! I'm glad to see you!"

Ewing's thin lips worked before he caught his voice. "What's the gun for, Nelson?"

Wayne lifted his gun in surprise. He had forgotten he held it. With a chuckle, he holstered it. "Not for you, Vance. Someone bushwhacked me, killed the team, nearly got me."

Vance's eyes grew cold and calculating but Wayne didn't notice as he pointed northward. He spoke excitedly, almost babbling. The law man swung out of the saddle. "Wait a minute, Nelson. You're not making sense. Tell me what happened."

Wayne caught himself. “Sure . . . but, first, did you just ride out from town?”

“Why?”

“Nothing’s happened there? To my place . . . or to Abbie?”

“No, everything’s all right.” He looked sharply at Wayne. “You could do with some rest—and some coffee. You can tell me what happened.”

He turned to his horse and tugged a roll from behind the cantle. He built a small fire and placed a stubby little coffee pot on the flames. Then he said, “Now, let me have it. Exactly what happened?”

Wayne described the ambush and the place. Vance listened, registering surprise and anger. He passed a cup of coffee to Wayne. “Have some. I’ll take you back to town before I head out for that wagon. Maybe I can pick up a trail.”

Wayne lowered the mug with a deep, contented sigh. Vance asked if Wayne had an idea, however slight, of the ambusher’s identity. “Those cartridge cases, maybe?”

“They could fit any one of a hundred rifles!”

Vance leaned forward, elbows on his knees. “Do you figure this has something to do with what’s been going on in town? What’s behind this, Nelson?”

“I . . . don’t know. Maybe he thought I was carrying something valuable.”

“Bullwash!”

"I—I've told you all I know."

Vance studied him and Wayne met his stare. At last Vance looked down at his cup with a deep sigh. "All right, I reckon you won't talk."

"I've told you—!"

"All you know. You never saw the gent. You have no idea who he is. That makes it damned nice and easy for him!" Vance came to his feet. "Pick up the gear while I check the horse—and my guns."

Vance stepped to the horse and checked the cinch, ran his hand down the animal's foreleg. Wayne kicked sand on the fire, bent to the blanket roll. Vance's lips peeled back in a tight smile as he pulled his Colt from its holster.

Wayne turned and Vance hastily swung open the loading gate of the weapon and appeared to check it, but he watched Wayne from under his brows. He'd let Wayne come within a few steps. He couldn't miss at that distance. A muscle moved in Ewing's cheek and his eyes gleamed.

Wayne moved toward him and he swung the load gate shut. The barrel was already pointed in Wayne's direction. A slight turn of the wrist, a pressure against the trigger and the third of them would—

He heard a faint jangle of trace chains. His head jerked up. Wayne came close, but over his shoulder Vance saw a boil of dust. A wagon came, fast. Wayne heard it now and swung around.

The fast-trotting team and big wagon came into view, Lew Kearney riding the high seat. Vance sucked in his breath and his face grew bleak. His eyes darted to the approaching wagon, to Wayne, to the wagon, and he slowly slid the gun into the holster.

Lew pulled up, kicked on the brake and jumped down. He ran to Wayne and grabbed him, a hand on each shoulder. "You're all right? My God, what happened back there!"

Wayne had to tell again about the ambush. "I'm still healthy, Lew—and lucky."

Lew stared at him in awe. "He could have killed you—or the desert."

Vance cut in. "I planned to ride Wayne into town, but I reckon you can take him now. If I can pick up trail right away, this gent might not have much of a lead. I sure as hell hope I catch up with him."

"Amen to that—in spades!" Wayne said.

Vance nodded curtly, strode back to his horse and swung into the saddle. He rode by them, lifted his hand in a curt salute and headed fast up the road toward the canyon. Both men watched him go. Lew shoved his hat back off his forehead. "Lucky you met up with him. He don't waste no time, does he?"

"No. Maybe he's all right, after all."

Even though Vance had assured Wayne that nothing had happened at home, Wayne still felt the urgent need to see for himself. It seemed an eternity before they threaded the hills bordering the Gila and saw the little town in the near distance. Wayne's eyes cast eastward toward his own place. They rattled by the Burrud house and came to Wayne's ranch.

Abbie appeared in the door as they rumbled into the yard, and ran out as Lew drew rein. Wayne jumped down and gathered her in, holding her close, looking at the solid, unharmed house. Abbie studied him with worried eyes. "Something terrible has happened. You're all right?"

"I'm fine. Something *tried* to happen."

She pulled him into the shadowy, cool kitchen before she would listen to his story. She said nothing, though her chin quivered a few times and her eyes brimmed. When Wayne finished, she came close, pulled his head to her body, her arms tight about his shoulders. Her voice caught. "The second try. Darling, we can't go on. We've got to do something! Maybe we could—"

She caught herself and threw a glance at Lew. Wayne understood—leave, run. She didn't want to say it in Lew's presence. She had given way to fear. He had faced ambush, alone, far away from any help and she believed it would happen again.

He smiled. "What will we do? Why, first, I'll report to Canby. Then I'll come back and rest."

"After that?"

He lightly touched her cheek. "He's missed me twice now, so we know he makes mistakes. He left a trail and Vance is following it. Maybe this time we'll catch him. His luck's running out, whoever he is." His voice deepened. "And you don't want to run any more than I do."

He left her to ride with Lew to the town and the freighting station. Lew wheeled the wagon into the big yard and Canby Tryon came bustling over as Lew reined in and Wayne jumped down. The little man's shrewd eyes swept over Wayne. "You look frazzled. What happened? Where's your outfit?"

Wayne told him, Lew adding confirmation. Canby listened and, when Wayne finished, glared across the yard. "No idea who it was? . . . and Vance is following trail now? Maybe he'll get somewhere, maybe he won't."

Wayne started, "I'm sorry about the horses—"

"So am I. You're a good freighter. But this is the second time someone has tried to cut you down. I have to figure he'll try again—no other way."

"Meaning what?"

"Meaning maybe next time he'll catch you with a full load. He might destroy the cargo. I can't afford that. I'm laying you off until this thing is cleared up."

Lew spoke angrily. "Canby, you can't do this to

Wayne! It ain't his fault. If you're doing this to him, then you can pay me off, too."

Canby had flushed a deep red but now his face lighted. "All right, Lew."

He paid them off and they were still somewhat dazed when they stepped out on the street. Wayne recovered first. "Well, that happened fast!"

"Fair takes your breath."

"He let you go because of Lorain. You gave him a real good excuse."

Lew nodded, looked sharply at Wayne. "What'll you do?"

"Work my place, like I've been wanting to."

Lew's eyes lighted. "Hey, Wayne! Canby did me a favor! I ain't beholden to him anymore! I can do as I please and see Lorain!"

"You can," Wayne said softly. "But don't forget—the killer might try for you next."

XIV

Lew struck Wayne lightly on the shoulder. “Don’t bury me yet. Maybe I’ll use this time to find him! Come on, let’s celebrate leaving Canby Tryon.”

He led the way to the Gila, a new spring in his step. As weary as Wayne felt, he had a new lift of spirits himself. After all that had happened, he needed a drink. The Gila had no customers. Joel Ramsey cleaned glassware behind the bar and his round face broke into a wide smile when they entered. Inez Vance played solitaire at a table close to the door that led to the living quarters.

She looked up, violet eyes hooded. Wayne instantly turned to her and, for a second, something like fear showed in her eyes though her face remained impassive, almost frozen. Wayne swept off his hat. “Mrs. Vance, I saw your husband this morning. He’s out on a trail. You ought to know—he saved my life. Someone tried to bushwhack me.”

Her eyes grew deeper but there was hardly any inflection in her voice. “I can see he failed. You have been lucky, Mr. Nelson.”

“I’ve got your husband to thank.”

“I’m sure Ewing will do all he can to take care of you, Mr. Nelson. He is a man who likes to finish what he starts. You can depend on him.”

She resumed her solitaire as if he had vanished. Wayne stood uncertain, a little irritated until he recalled the stories of her strangeness, then he joined Lew at the bar.

Inez continued her play. She covertly watched the two men, listening to their talk. Her calm face registered no emotion but she made three misplays in succession. She swept up the cards and dealt again. She learned the men had just lost their jobs at Canby Tryon's because of what had happened to Wayne.

Inez listened and played. Twice her lips flattened and she paused with a card held over the table, but she quickly continued the play. She learned what Nelson and Kearney planned to do.

Wayne refused Lew's offer of a second drink. He told Joel he'd come back tonight in the hope that Vance would return with definite news. Joel's moon face grew serious. "If anyone can catch that sidewinder, it's Ewing Vance."

The two men left. Inez abruptly swept up the cards, started for the door near her, checked and looked over her shoulder at Joel. She returned slowly to the bar and spoke in a friendly voice. "Mr. Nelson had a narrow escape." Joel nodded and she smiled. "They're good friends of yours. Old friends, perhaps?"

"Well, in a way of speaking."

Her voice warmed. "I believe you came to Florence with them, didn't you? Let's see, I remember, nine of you came together. Tell me about yourself, Joel, Ewing never has."

Inez enjoyed his secretive squirming, forced him to reveal things, little by little. Not that she learned very much, but Joel sweated, sought escape but could find none.

"All of you were soldiers? I wonder if any of you saw service in Arkansas or Missouri. I heard there was a lot of fighting there."

Joel frowned. "I can't figure why you'd be interested."

She laughed. "Actually, I'm just curious. I heard a man talking about it several months ago."

"Who?" he asked sharply.

"I don't know. He was traveling through to Phoenix. I haven't seen him since. Are you sure none of your friends—?"

"Real sure, Ma'am."

"But you've known them all for so long and for so many years!"

"All but Wayne. We met him in Texas."

He missed the flick of her eyes. "Then maybe he—"

"Not him. He was in Virginia the whole of the war—four years of it. Now, Ma'am, I really got to get whiskey stock to the bar."

She walked away, entered the living area and closed the door behind her. Joel mopped sweat from his forehead. He looked at the closed door.

Questions! Questions! But he hadn't told her a thing.

Late in the afternoon, three heavily armed, fast-riding men came into town from three directions, converging on the stage station. Each dismounted, lifted heavy saddlebags from his mount and disappeared inside. Each came out empty-handed, the strain lines easing from his dust-streaked face as he headed for the Gila.

They were gold riders from the mines. The express company was not responsible for bullion until it was delivered to its stations and a receipt was issued. So these men rode swift as an arrow from mine to the nearest stage depot. They never took the same route twice or held to the same schedule. Their cargo in the express company strongbox, they could shed responsibility and seek cheer at the Gila or Madam Verona's.

Just before the supper hour, Vic Hayes left the stage station, holding himself to a saunter, although excitement roweled him. He walked to the livery stable to find Hal Grayson considering a horse being offered for sale. Vic spoke casually to his friend. "I got a full bottle. Drop around when you finish your business if you feel like it."

Grayson caught the slight accent, looked up quickly and nodded. Hayes wandered off. Once in his house, he sailed his hat toward a wall hook then stared about the room. He walked to the table and sat down, sprawling back in his chair, frowning at the far wall.

Hard blue eyes looked slowly about, dwelling an instant on each bit of furniture as if he set them deep in his memory against a time he'd see them no more. With an impatient grunt, he arose, crossed to a cupboard and pulled out a bottle of whiskey.

A moment later there was a knock on the door and Hayes jumped slightly. He yanked it open and admitted Grayson, who asked, "What's up, Vic?"

"I promised you whiskey."

He closed the door behind Grayson, who moved over to the table and sat down. As Grayson poured the drinks, Hayes found paper and pencil and came to the table. He took the drink Grayson had poured and tossed it down.

Grayson said evenly, "It ain't only the whiskey, Vic."

Hays laughed. "No. It's plenty of money and a chance to get out of this town. The bullion just came in from the mines. It leaves before dawn tomorrow—special run. You 'n me—we'll get it."

Grayson's eyes widened and his lips parted, then he snapped them shut. He swallowed then hastily seized his glass. Hayes drew lines on the paper, then an X and drew a circle about it. He pushed it to Grayson. "Right there, Hal. You be there—marked. Throw down on us. I'll see that the driver makes no gun play. You'll take the strongbox. Then—"

"Vic, we can't do this."

The two big men looked at one another across the table. Finally Grayson's eyes slid away and a flush touched his neck. He said stubbornly, "We just can't, Vic."

"Now wait a minute! We've talked this over and you agreed to the whole deal."

"Sure, but I was mad—at Hank Malloy. No, I . . ."

"Now you're scared?" Hayes asked. Grayson's head jerked up, eyes sparking. Hayes smiled. "Hell, I know better! It must be something else."

"I just can't do it. It's all wrong—you 'n me outlaws."

Hayes studied Grayson. He eased back in his chair. "I reckon it *is* all wrong, Hal. But there's something that's worse. I don't see how you could forget it."

He leaned across the table, pointed toward the window. "You know what's at the edge of town, Hal. A cemetery. Bedford Drumbo's out there, and Skip Adams. If they could talk, they'd tell you what's worse. Point is, they can't—ever again. They're dead. They can't do nothing but rot down in that damn desert sand. Ever wonder what it feels like to be dead, Hal?" His voice shivered. "I have. Now we've gone over all the arguments. We've got no chance unless we take this one. Neither of us wants to be out there with Bed and Skip . . . or the other five that're bound to join 'em."

"But—"

Vic cut in, voice tight and fierce. "Bullion in the strongbox, Hal—thousands of dollars! And it's ours, simple and easy."

He shoved the map at Grayson and tapped the circle. "Listen how easy. You be right here. No trouble. We'll dump the strongbox and then I'll make the driver head on south instead of back here. That gives you plenty of time. I'll come back with a posse, of course. But I'll see to it that they'll pick up a wrong trail."

"But what about the bullion?"

"You'll bury the gold—close by, but don't leave any traces. Then show up here and act as usual. After I come back from leading the posse to hell and gone on a wild goose chase, we'll just sit around a few days."

Hayes hitched forward. "Who'll tie us in with it? We'll ride out, dig up the gold and head south. It's not too far to the border. Think of it, Hal! What will that gold do for us in Mexico or South America? We'll live like kings . . . be big men!" His voice lowered. "We'll *live,* man, not get a knife or a bullet in the back."

Grayson caught the fever, the glowing picture. He looked out the window. There was a scabrous adobe shack across the street and the barren earth about it, the earth that held Bed and Skip could hold him. "Let's go over it, Vic. I want to make sure."

Late that night, Wayne nursed along a couple of drinks and listened to the flow of talk in the saloon. Word had spread, evidently from Canby, about his ambush and he had been forced to describe it half a dozen times. Now he felt the uselessness of waiting. Obviously, Vance was still on the trail. He said as much to Frank Burrud, who nodded and the two men pushed back from the table.

Inez Vance, who had surprisingly remained in the saloon most of the evening, looked up from her table by the door. "You're not going to wait, Mr. Nelson? I'm sure Ewing will come any time."

"It's late and—"

She suddenly looked beyond him and spoke calmly, "Here he is now."

Vance came through the batwings. Dust covered his clothing and he showed the strain of the day. Talk ceased as he swiped his free hand across his dry lips and advanced to the bar. Then Wayne recognized the thing Vance held in his hand. "A bow! Frank, he's got an Indian bow!"

He and Frank pushed forward, shoving men aside. Joel poured a drink for the law man, who placed the bow on the bar. Wayne and Frank pushed up beside him and he placed a hand on the weapon as he tossed down his drink. Others pressed close, eager and curious. He turned and lifted the bow. "Has anyone ever seen this before?"

The wood was smooth and dark, shaped to graceful, flowing lines. The grip was made of horn and the string was gut. The weapon was functional, plain except for crude decorations about the grip and markings where the wood had been notched for the string. A whiskered man looked closely at it. "Sure that's Injun?"

Vance looked startled. "What else could it be?"

"There ain't no tribes in these parts use a bow like that. The markings and shape is all wrong."

"Eastern, maybe?" Frank asked.

Vance grunted. "It could be Fijian for all I care! I want to know if anyone has seen this before."

There was a chorus of dissent. Wayne broke in. "Where'd you find it, Vance?"

The marshal turned to him. "First, I'd better tell you what happened to your bushwhacker."

"You found him!"

"No. I found the trail where you said I would. I've been following it ever since. I lost sign at least half a dozen times but always managed to pick it up. It went every direction of the compass for a time, then headed directly south."

Vance savored the rapt, tense attention. "Once

he figured he was safe, that bushwhacker headed straight for home. The trail led me to the Gila, not far from your place, Burrud. Sign ended right at the edge of the water so I figured he swum his horse across. I did the same and cast around for sign this side of the river. Didn't find any. I figure now he went upstream and came out close to the road on the same side where he went in. Once he hit the bridge and road, there'd be no chance of trailing him." Vance's hand slapped the bow. "But I did find this."

"Then it *was* a fire arrow," Wayne said softly. "Malloy couldn't quite believe it."

"I didn't quite believe it, either. But I eat crow now. This proves it."

"But who does it belong to? If that bushwhacker was trailed to the road right at the edge of town—"

"Then he's close around," Vance snapped. "I figure he used this bow. I'll find him if I have to turn the whole town upside down!"

His voice rang with determination.

There was little more he could tell them and he was obviously tired. He pushed through the crowd toward his quarters. He was halted by the manager of the express company, who whispered something. Vance grimaced, nodded curtly, and they parted.

Later that night, Vance lay stretched out on the bed, contented with the meal Inez had cooked, the whiskey on the table beside him, pleased with himself. Inez sat at the dresser, brushing her long black hair. The lamp made lovely highlights on the angles of her face. Vance eyed the faint and uncertain outline of her beautiful body beneath the ugly folds of her voluminous gown.

He suddenly became aware that she studied him closely in her mirror. Their eyes met. She spoke with a throaty finality. "You're a fool, Ewing."

He folded his hands across his stomach and saw the shadow of her breast as she lifted her arm. "Strong words, Inez."

She swung to face him, violet eyes sparking. "That bow—it's a long and foolish chance."

He laughed. "Think a minute. It's been in the back of our closet since we brought it from Kentucky. I haven't used it in all that time. No one here has ever seen it." His voice grew smug. "But I hadn't lost the touch. The arrow went exactly where I aimed."

He reached for the whiskey. "I don't take chances. Maybe by some accident the bow would be found in that closet. How would you explain it? Now I've shown it around. Nobody recognizes it . . . and it's back in the closet. Nobody suspects us. Would anyone believe a man would show a weapon that can hang him? I did—and got away with it."

Inez considered, head tilting slightly. She took a new tack. "Did you have to say that you followed a trail right here to town? Couldn't you have said you lost it somewhere in the desert?"

He swung out of the bed and came toward her. She watched. Something in her eyes made him stop just beyond arm's reach. He shrugged. "Drumbo and Adams died here, so no one is surprised. Besides, I got to show that I'm working on this thing. I've been holed up in the hills beyond the river, waiting for dark. That's when I got the idea about the bow."

The brush lay in her lap as she studied him with the dawning of new respect. "When did you get the bow?"

"Rode in after dark. Came in the back way and got it. Then I walked around the building and in the batwings—as easy as that!"

Another idea brought her head up in a new anger. "You failed again with Nelson."

He wheeled back to the bottle. "Yes, damn his luck! Had him right in the sights and he jerked just as I pulled the trigger."

"You could have been seen."

His smugness returned. "I took care of that. When I saw I couldn't get him out from behind that wagon, I shot his horse and pulled out. The next morning I headed back to meet him on the road. I'd have shot him then if Kearney hadn't come along."

She spoke dryly. "You have no luck with him. Better leave Nelson alone for a while." Her voice tightened. "But only for a while. He has to go, along with the others."

Vance studied her, again struck by this insatiable thing that had seized her. He spoke shortly. "Don't worry. You'll tick him off with the rest."

"You promised them you'd find the killer. How can you? Turn yourself in?"

He burst into laughter. "Hardly! The last one on the list will die when I shoot him for resisting arrest for the murder of all the others."

"Yes, that will be true justice. Edward would like that." His face subtly changed. She sensed his irritation. "You're doing well, Ewing. I'm proud of you. But maybe you'd best do nothing more for a while. You can't afford another slip—like Nelson."

He responded swiftly to what he believed was her consideration and worry for him. He stepped closer, bent down. "I won't fail with the next one. It'll be soon. I've picked him."

"Who?"

"You'll see. You'll enjoy it more that way."

He kissed her. She quickly turned her head and his lips touched her cheek. With an instinctive gesture, she brushed his moist hand from her breast and turned back to the mirror.

He stood for a long moment, looking down at the dark crown of her head. The silver brush moved in unhurried rhythm but her slender shoulders were set and tense. He looked at the unemotional, beautiful mask of her face in the glass. Her eyes were distant and impersonal.

He turned back to the table. After another drink, he dropped onto the bed, barred and cheated. Then his confidence returned. He rolled over on his side to seek sleep. Tomorrow would be busy.

She'd change—as she had after Drumbo and Adams had died.

There had been excited talk with the Burruds all the way home about the finding of the bow, and Wayne repeated the story to Abbie. She, too, felt the excitement and agreed that Ewing Vance had certainly stirred himself. She and Wayne were both keyed up when they went to bed. Abbie's voice came out of the darkness. "Wayne, that bow."

"What about it?"

"Vance found it down by the river. Didn't you and Frank and Jesse check all over the ground down there the morning after the fire? I wonder how you missed it."

"I guess it was pretty well hidden. Vance was luckier."

She turned over and soon her regular breathing told Wayne she slept. He was drowsy and his mind moved in a slow, sluggish way. Funny about that bow. He pictured the Burrud farm the morning after the fire. He pictured the search out from the barn down to and along the river bank. One of you should have found that bow! his mind sluggishly told him.

He seemed to argue with a dream image of himself. But we did look—good. Then how come Vance found it? I don't know. Find out. I will, tomorrow, when I go to town. I'll ask him. He drifted off to sleep.

In that darkest period of the night just before dawn, there were furtive sounds beyond the lowered blinds of the stage station. Within, the express company manager watched the placing of gold bars in the strong box. Vic Hayes and the office clerk finally stepped back and the manager dropped the heavy lid, snapped the lock. Ewing Vance, who had been leaning on the near end of the counter, glanced at the clock.

The manager said, "A hell of a note, Ewing, after the day you had. But the gold came in from the mines and none of us feel safe until it's on its way to Tucson,"

"When will you leave?"

"Just before dawn." The manager looked at Hayes. "Better get some breakfast, Vic. Andy Jefford's driving this trip. He'll be in soon to hitch up."

Vance offered, "I'll stick around and check over the passengers."

"No passengers on this run, Ewing. No one but us knows it's going. You get to bed. I'll keep watch until Vic and Andy drive out."

Vance yawned, flipped a hand in farewell and eased out the door that was quickly locked behind him. He shuffled off, until he was around the corner. Then he threw a quick look over his shoulder.

The first glimmer of the idea had come when the manager had stopped him in the saloon last night. Armed law always stood by while the gold was transferred, and waited until the special stage left. Now, because of the manager's offer, Vance had over an hour, maybe two in which to act.

He moved down the dark street, circled the saloon and unlocked the back door. He eased into the kitchen, crossed it to the bedroom. He found the lamp, lit it, and Inez instantly sat up, awake.

He went to the big clothes press, spoke to her over his shoulder as he pulled out shirt, pants, another hat. "Make some coffee . . . and sandwiches. I want to get out of here soon."

"Something wrong?"

"Not for us, sweetheart. For someone else."

She picked up a robe and went into the kitchen. Vance checked his cartridge loops and his Colt, dropped rifle shells in a pocket. Picking up the clothes, he went to the kitchen and tied them with a length of twine. Then he went to the stable.

When he returned, coffee and a sandwich waited on the table while Inez wrapped two more and placed them beside him. She sat down across the table to her own coffee, asked a tentative question but Vance was pleasantly secretive. She was excited. Ewing was going to get another of those murderers! She could feel it.

He finished his coffee standing up, glanced at the clock and hastily reached for the rifle scabbard on the wall. Her brooding eyes followed him to the door, where he stopped.

"If anyone asks for me, say I left early for the other side of the river to pick up any more sign. I'll be back at noon, if not before."

She quietly said two words. "Don't miss."

He was momentarily startled and then he opened the door and stepped outside. Inez remained at the table. She turned her head when she heard the soft beat of hoofs that swiftly faded away. Then her hand, lying supine on the table, slowly turned and the tapering fingers formed a fist, the wrist cords standing out.

The marshal rode north, a faint glint of starlight on the badge on his shirt. Far out beyond the town, he started a huge circle that would take him around the town and southward.

Vic Hayes also sat eating at a table, Grayson across from him. The lamplight played on the two men, accenting Grayson's set expression. He looked like a man who drove himself to an unpleasant task.

Hayes shoveled in more fried egg, washed it down with a swig of coffee. "It's all set, Hal. You know exactly where to go and what to do. Andy Jerrod's driving and he's an old woman. He'll probably keel right over when you throw down on us."

"I still don't like it."

"Damn it, Hal! Can't I depend on you? Who

knows when they'll make another bullion shipment?"

"All right!"

"Just pop up over the rim, fire in the air and throw down on us. We'll drive off lickety-split after we've pitched out the strongbox. I know Andy! I'll keep him going south—and there's nothing between here and Tucson. You know what to do?"

"I know."

"Don't stretch your time too thin. Better head out. I'll see you after the show."

Grayson arose with an air of final decision. He also picked up a rifle in the corner and eased out into the night. Not long after, he rode south through the darkness. Far ahead, Vance Ewing rode steadily at an easy canter.

As the first faint light touched the east, Vance came to one of the innumerable dry washes that crossed the road. Here, the stage would slow as the horses picked their way into the rough, sandy bed and up the far bank. On the far side, to the west, was a little knoll crowned with a tangle of mesquite and ocotillo. A man there would never be seen from the road.

Vance rode along the wash for a hundred yards before he crossed. At this distance from the road, no one would notice fresh tracks. He drifted up to the foot of the knoll and dismounted, ground-tying the horse. He climbed the slight ascent and looked down the far slope. He checked the sweep of the road, the dip into the wash, the steep lift on this side. He considered the best place for the job. Right in the middle of the wash, he decided. Be more confusion there.

Satisfied, he descended the slope and pulled the bundle of clothes from behind the cantle. He swiftly changed, made up the new bundle and replaced it. He pulled the horse further back to another clump of mesquite and tethered it. Then he took the rifle from the scabbard, levered a shell into the chamber and returned to the crest of the knoll.

He eased down behind the mesquite, looked out at the road and, satisfied, made himself comfortable. The rifle lay across one arm. He looked at the sky, still dark except for the ghostly light just above the eastern horizon. By the time the stage arrived, everything would be crystal clear.

He wriggled into a more comfortable position and let his thoughts wander. Maybe Inez was right, after this he should let things quiet down. She worried about him and that in itself marked a great change. He was beginning to crack through that cold shell, push Edward's memory into the background. How long and how many ways he had tried to do that! Then the nine men rode in and he had found—

He froze, hearing a sound from the north. He

threw a startled look at the half dark sky. Had the stage left town ahead of time! This light would be tricky. He dropped flat and lifted the rifle. The sound came closer, then a single horse and rider loomed out of the shadows beyond the wash.

Vance lowered the rifle and strained to see. The man descended into the wash, moved unhurriedly across and ascended the near bank. A steel shoe clanked against rock and the man was directly below Vance.

A large man, he could see that, but the hat brim made the face invisible. The man continued southward and soon the last sound faded. Vance came to his feet, stared southward, strained to hear. There was nothing more. Vance stood uncertain. Then he looked at the sky again and his breathing calmed.

There was no further sign or sound. The man had ridden with a purpose as though he had a long way to go. Vance considered. It would be at least an hour before the stage arrived and by then the single, early morning traveler would be well beyond hearing a single rifle shot. Vance stretched out again, the rifle ready to hand.

The light increased. There was a brilliant brightness to the world, a false polish that the heat would soon dispel. Vance could command the whole of the road, clearly see the wheel ruts in the wash. The soft colors of the morning sky blended and vanished as the brassy sun lifted to the horizon.

He heard the sound of traces and his eyes grew cold and narrow as he put the rifle to shoulder and rested his cheek along the stock. The sounds vibrated along the ground—six horses moving in unison. He heard the rumble of the wheels.

The coach appeared exactly above his rifle sights. He saw Andy Jeffords, arms extended to the reins, foot resting on the board by the brake. Beside him, Vic Hayes swayed to the swing of the coach, scattergun cradled in his arms.

The rifle sights picked up Hayes' broad chest, dipped as the vehicle dropped into the bed of the wash. Andy cracked the whip and the horses strained against the pull of the sand on the wheels. The thin black slice of the front sights rested on the left pocket of Hayes' shirt, moved a fraction to the right and steadied. The muzzle followed the coach as it neared the center of the wash. Vance's finger tightened on the trigger, slowly, evenly squeezed back.

The rifle's report was a flat smack, as though someone had snapped a dry board. A thin wisp of blue smoke drifted across the sight. Vic Hayes jerked convulsively, half rose, pitched straight forward off the seat, under the wheels of the coach. Andy Jefford's bearded face showed stunned surprise.

Vance slid down the back slope, came to his

feet and raced to his horse. He shoved the rifle in the scabbard and swung into the saddle. He jerked the horse around and set spurs. The animal raced westward. Vance reining around low hummocks the better to hide himself from the road. Then he headed south, leaving a clear trail.

Free of the little hills about the wash, he set spurs, leaning into the wind. He threw a quick look over his shoulder but there was no sign of pursuit. He smiled tightly and faced forward again.

Suddenly he caught movement ahead, off the road. A lone rider topped a rise, so distant that no features could be distinguished. Vance savagely swung the horse to the right and pulled his hat brim low. He saw the distant rider halt but Vance raked the spurs. Soon he was out of sight, but a sickening dread that he might have been recognized even at a distance swept over him. It must have been that lone rider he had seen earlier—or maybe another. Either way, it was bad enough.

He raced on, knowing he had to carry this through, even with a bluff. His fear waned as his brain clicked into cold, precise weighing of the situation. He reined in, knowing the horse could not keep up this speed in the growing heat. He leaned on the saddle horn and considered. Confidence returned. He could not have been recognized at that distance. Satisfied, he rode on, now taking care to hide his trail.

At long last he came to the river far to the west of the town. He swam his horse and disappeared into the low hills on the northern bank. He dismounted and changed his clothes. When he swung into the saddle again, his rifle was cleaned and he wore his familiar clothes, the law badge glinting in the sun. He rode directly eastward to the road.

He rode without hurry back into town. He could not help a sharp, searching look down the street and gave a soft sigh when he saw that the stage had not yet returned. He took his time in the stable, unsaddling, watering, and feeding the horse. Unhurriedly, he crossed the yard and entered the kitchen. He heard Inez stir in the living room and he hung his rifle in its usual place on the wall before he went in.

Inez, sewing by the window, looked at him. She caught his smile, his air of expectancy. She dropped the sewing in her lap and her lips parted, her eyes lighted. "Someone else?"

"Vic Hayes . . . for good."

He came toward her but she made a gesture toward the door that led to the saloon. "Better get in there. Wayne Nelson has been asking for you."

He stopped short. "How long?"

"Half an hour, maybe. No longer."

Vance wondered what Nelson could want of

him. More about that ambush, probably, and he'd have to make up his story of casting about for trail all morning. He discovered his palms were sweaty and he rubbed them along his trouser legs.

Inez saw his nervousness. "No one saw you when—?"

"No one. I'll see Nelson."

He opened the door and stepped into the saloon. Joel stood behind the bar, talking to Nelson and, at a far corner table, a lone drinker played solitaire as he nursed his shot of whiskey along. Wayne turned when he saw Joel look beyond him. Ewing Vance closed the door behind him and Wayne noticed the dust on his clothing.

Vance came up to the bar. "I just come from beyond the river looking for that bushwhacker of yours."

"Any luck?"

"Scoured the hills . . . nothing." Vance wearily signaled Joel for a drink. "I hear you've been asking for me. You forgot to tell me something about the ambush?"

"No, it's about that bow."

"The bow!" Vance hid his sudden start. "What about it?"

"It keeps bothering me. The Burruds and I went all over that ground. I can't see how in the hell we missed it."

"There's a million places to hide anything around your spread."

"Sure, but—Just exactly where was it, Vance?"

"Why as to that, it's pretty hard to say. One saguaro looks like another. Let's see now if I can tell you exactly."

He frowned, masking his effort to beat down panic. His brain moved swiftly and coldly, picturing the location of the barn he had fired, his line of retreat. How could he describe a specific section of river bank that he had not seen? He scratched his head. "By God, Wayne, I don't know that I *could* tell you. I could take you right to the spot better than—"

A loud shout came from the street. Vance looked toward the door, glad of the interruption. "Now what in hell has happened?"

The batwings burst open as a man plunged inside. He looked wildly around, saw Vance. "Marshal! Come quick!"

"What is it?"

"They tried to hold up the stage. Vic Hayes is dead!"

XVI

Wayne raced at Ewing's heels out into the street. Men converged on the stage station but the crowd parted as Vance and Wayne came up. Andy Jerrod, hat pushed back from his seamed face, spoke to the express manager. Hal Grayson, face pale, nodded wordlessly as the manager looked at him for confirmation. Wayne's eyes swept over the coach, searching for the bullet scars of a hold-up, but the smooth finish was untouched.

Jerrod said, "Apache Wash. Just one shot—Vic made a funny sound and pitched forward. Come so fast I—run over him."

Vance asked swift questions and Jerrod gave him the full details. Beads of sweat stood on Hal Grayson's forehead. Wayne looked within the coach. Vic Hayes lay on the floor and there had been some attempt to decently arrange him. Dust and abrasions covered his face and there was a dark stain on his chest. Wayne dropped back and turned his head, swallowing hard.

"Hold-up's what I figured first," Jerrod finished. "But no one showed. There was just the one shot, nothing else."

"The strongbox?" Vance asked.

"Still right in the boot. That's why I come back here."

Vance turned to Grayson. "Where do you come in, Hal?"

Wayne caught a fleeting, fearful expression in Grayson's eyes. But it was gone as Grayson moistened his lips. "I'd gone south—to see about some horses. I guess I left just before the stage and didn't know it. I'd pulled in to check a shoe and was just ready to ride on when I heard the shot."

"You were that close!"

"It was some way off, back of me. Out there, it could mean someone in trouble. You know, Indians, or a man hurt . . . or lost."

"So you went back?"

"After I thought about it."

"See anything?"

"Saw a rider heading fast toward me. About that time, he saw me and veered off, headed west. He sure didn't want me to get a good look at him."

"Did you?"

Something in Vance's tone made Wayne look sharply at the law man but his face was expressionless. Grayson shook his head. "He was too far off. I couldn't see much more 'n the horse. No, I couldn't say who he was."

"Too bad."

"But, funny thing, Vance, seemed like I ought to have known him. Fairly tall, I'd say—if you could judge a man that far away."

"Something you recognized?"

"No, something in the set of him. Maybe it's just imagination."

"Probably." Vance looked at the crowd. "Andy, you come inside the station. I want to ask you some questions. Better get the strongbox back in the safe."

Grayson asked, "What about Vic?"

"We'll get him to the undertaker. I just don't understand this. Did someone plan to rob the stage and then lose his nerve? I'll get out there and pick up trail as quick as I can."

Someone went for the undertaker and the express company employees unloaded the strongbox. A knot of the curious still remained but Wayne moved off.

He walked slowly back to the saloon, preceded by a few excited men. He stood at the bar nursing a drink, half listening to the excited talk and speculation. Then he took bottle and glass and moved over to a distant table.

The initial shock of Vic Hayes' death started to wane. Attempted hold-up? Perhaps, what with the express company strongbox on this extra, no-passenger run. Someone could have learned about it. Maybe the shot had been intended only as a warning but had accidentally killed Vic. Then the robber had lost his nerve.

But Wayne had a grim conviction this was another in a series of killings designed to wipe out nine men. Three of them gone now—six to go. Hold-up? . . . or murder? One shot only. The shotgun guard gone, the looting of the stage would have been easy. So that wasn't the point. Wayne's fingers tightened around his glass as he reached the inevitable conclusion—murder.

Hal Grayson pushed open the batwings and walked heavily to the bar, avoiding the other men by moving to the far end. Wayne wondered if Hal also felt this was more than robbery. Joel served whiskey and Grayson tossed the drink, poured another and immediately tossed it down.

Joel, distraught, asked a question in a low voice. Grayson's voice lifted. "Damn it! I don't know a thing!"

Joel jerked back in hurt surprise. Grayson swiped his hand across his eyes. "Hell, Joel! forget it. This whole thing has got me edgy."

"Sure, Hal. Wayne's got a table to himself over there. He won't ask questions."

Grayson swept up his bottle and glass and came over. Wayne pushed out a chair and Grayson thudded into it. "No questions."

"None," Wayne agreed.

Grayson poured a drink, studied the amber in the glass. His forehead creased in ridges and his eyes grew somber and withdrawn. Wayne said nothing as Grayson scowled at his drink. Finally, he finished it. He threw an almost frightened look at Wayne and refilled his glass. Wayne let him alone, looking across the room to the bar. The batwings swung open and a new group came in, saw Grayson and came to the table. Grayson made as if to leave, but he could not. A man asked, "What happened out there, Hal?"

"Hear you got there right away?"

"Where was Hayes then? How'd you find him?"

"No sign of them robbers?"

Grayson jerked to his feet, nearly tipping the bottle. He righted it, something wild in his eyes. "There's nothing I can tell you. Got to get out of here. Wayne, how about you?"

Wayne instantly stood up. "Save your questions, boys. Hal and me—we've lost a good friend. Maybe later, huh?"

"Why, sure, Wayne."

"Never thought about it that way. Sorry, Hal."

Grayson brushed them aside and, with a curt signal to Wayne strode out of the saloon. The street had returned to normal. Wayne had time for only a brief glimpse, for Grayson set a fast and angry pace, growling, "Vultures! They want to pick the thing over and tear it apart. Why can't they leave it alone!"

"Excited," Wayne replied. "Like we would be if it was someone else."

Grayson threw him an angry look but remained tight-faced and silent all the way to his place. He unlocked the door, grunted an invitation to enter, and strode in. He disappeared through a doorway, returned with bottle and glasses, thumped them on the table. "Help yourself."

Wayne shook his head. Grayson poured a stiff drink, swallowed half of it. He sat down, fidgeted and then came to his feet again. He wheeled on Wayne. "Vic . . . I . . . Oh, hell! What's the use? There's nothing to say."

He circled the table and stood at the window, hands clasping and unclasping behind his back. His face looked stone carved. Wayne poured a small drink, more to keep from looking at Grayson as he spoke. "Sometimes it's best to talk, Hal, or you explode."

Grayson whipped around. "About what! Go over what I've already told a dozen people?"

"No—about what you didn't tell them."

Grayson lunged to the table, leaned on it, towering over Wayne. "What do you know?"

"Not a thing, Hal. Something's eating you and it's more than Vic's death. Tell me if you want—or don't tell me."

Grayson remained motionless, finally sighed, circled the table and sat down again. "I wasn't looking for horses this morning, Wayne. I went out there for another reason. Can I trust you?"

"You'll have to decide that."

Grayson closed his eyes as he spoke. "When these killings started, Vic and me didn't want to stay here. We wanted to get out while we were alive and start somewhere else."

"I know."

"But the rest of you were against it and that sort of held us back. Vic knew about these special bullion shipments. They carry enough to set us both up if we could pull it off and get out of the country. So we planned to get the next shipment—the one that went out this morning."

Wayne sat like a man of stone. "Then you were the one who—?"

"No! I was exactly where I said I was—clean down the road. It was the place Vic and me had picked."

Wayne listened as he told of their plans, first in shock and then in a peculiar twisted pity. Grayson was caught in his own trap. Vic Hayes had been destroyed by it. Grayson finished, "I heard the shot, just like I said. I couldn't figure it. Maybe Vic had signaled me, or Jerrod had caught on somehow—I don't know. I rode back. That's the gospel truth, but who'd believe me?"

Wayne said thoughtfully, "If the strongbox was gone, no one would. But there's no need to worry about it. You didn't rob the stage. You didn't shoot Vic."

Grayson hid his face in his hands. "But I feel like I did! Vic might be alive. It's like I pulled the trigger."

"Hal, the main thing is you didn't. But there's something a hell of a lot more important."

Grayson looked up. "More important?"

"Even if you hadn't planned to rob the stage, would Vic still have rode shotgun? . . . Then someone waited at Apache Wash to kill Vic. He made sure of his shot and then ran. No other way to figure it."

"Then the man I saw . . . !"

"The killer. Couldn't be anyone else. He's the one who got Drumbo and Skip—now Vic. Three of us gone, Hal. Who's next? That's the main thing."

Grayson sucked in his breath. "Me! That's who's next! I had a glimpse of him. He knew I saw him."

"Now wait. You could be right, but he'll lay low until the excitement has died down. By then we'll figure out something."

"Have we so far!"

"Maybe not, but don't you run, Hal. Everyone thinks this was a try at robbery, including Vance. You run, and they'll tag you with it—and probably hang you for shooting Vic."

"Oh, Lord!"

Wayne arose. "Just go about your business and keep quiet. I won't tell anyone, not even Abbie. Strange how this worked out. You're innocent of crime, and you can thank a cold-blooded murder for it. You're lucky—Vic wasn't. He's dead."

He walked out leaving the man unmoving, a frozen figure at the table.

On the way home, Wayne stopped and told the Burruds about the killing, omitting all reference to Grayson's revelation. He told them his own suspicions. He left them silently asking one another his own question. Who is next?

At home, he told Abbie. He did not mention his own thoughts but he sensed that she understood. She looked frightened, but her chin firmed as she turned to the stove. The meal was broken now and then they forced conversation. They busied themselves with minor chores and then prepared for bed. Just as he was about to blow out the lamp, Abbie suddenly remembered. "What did Vance say about the bow?"

"The bow? The bow! Abbie, I clean forgot it!"

A few hours later, Ewing Vance bolted the door between the saloon and the living quarters. He went into the kitchen and returned with bottle and glass, put them down on the table where Edward's picture sat. He looked irritably at it. "A poor place for that picture."

Inez calmly looked up from her sewing. "Who sees it?"

"Someone might."

"I'll put it back on the dresser." She made another stitch, looked up. "You've taken to drinking that stuff instead of selling it."

"I've ridden all over hot hell and you begrudge

me a drink! What kind of a woman are you?"

She didn't take umbrage. "Vic Hayes—that's good. But you nearly got caught. How did it happen?"

He still felt shaky inside. He started to speak of it, changed his mind. Instead, he told her of the killing. She dropped the sewing in her lap and listened, enthralled. Her lips parted and a glow came deep in her eyes. When he came to his near encounter with Hal Grayson, her expression subtly became stony and uncaring.

He finished, taking a drink. "It scared me. I've been chasing my own shadow ever since. I'll make up some story about finding a trail and then losing it."

"Three of them!" she breathed. She eagerly faced him. "And the next—when?"

"When! I don't know. Didn't you hear me? I nearly got caught today!"

"You weren't. Grayson was too far away to know you."

"I wish I could be bottom certain. And Wayne Nelson is asking questions about that damn bow—where I found it and how come he and the Burruds missed it. I'd better let things ease off."

"This is no time to get weak-kneed, Ewing. If you think Grayson might recognize you, get him—and quick."

"But—"

"And the others." Exultation touched her, lifted

hand clenched in a fist at her breast. "Wayne Nelson first. He wasn't at Lawrence, but—"

"Inez! Nelson wasn't at Lawrence?"

"I pumped Joel Ramsey. They picked Nelson and his wife up on the trail—somewhere in Texas."

"You knew this, Inez? You didn't tell me? And I've tried for him twice! Wouldn't eight deaths be enough? If he wasn't at Lawrence—"

"Don't be a fool!" she said scathingly. "He's like the rest. Besides, he is asking questions. You've already marked him and you've failed twice. He's looking for you. No, he must go."

Ewing reached for the bottle but pulled his hand back. He studied the intense glow in her face. She had the appearance of a woman at the peak of passion. He felt a sickness in his stomach and the enormity of what he had already done pressed on him. He took a deep, shuddering breath. "I believe you like this—beyond evening the score for Edward. You like to see men die."

"They have to die—all of them."

Ewing stood before her, looking at her with dawning horror. He shook his head as though to clear his brain. She looked up and, once more, the full power of her beauty hit him, the elusive thing that was the real Inez and that he had never quite been able to capture.

He moistened his lips. "Inez, I . . . Three of them, Inez. Won't that pay for Edward? For you and me? This has changed us. I have to force myself to face people. I can't be easy with anyone, anymore. I have to watch everything I do and say."

She waited. He spread his hands. "I'm jumpy. I've got to keep thinking all the time, or I'll slip and they'll hang me. This is changing you, too, Inez. It was bad enough before, but this is worse. Why, we're murderers—three times over!"

"But we've kept our promise to Edward. He must be happy."

His anger broke and he struck his chest with his fist. "Edward! Edward! He's happy! But I'm not! I can't go on. It has to stop—it has stopped!"

Her face changed. The angles at cheek, jaw, and chin became prominent as the smooth skin tightened over the bones. She considered him with a mixture of anger and contempt—and something akin to wildness.

"No! The rest must go, all of them—and *you'll* do it. You don't dare do anything else. I'll see to it. One word, one whisper and they'll know. You'll get them all—or you'll hang."

His eyes bugged out. He saw her without the mask of beauty and desire, looked into murky depths he had not believed existed, or had refused to see because of his own infatuation.

"You'd do this! You've driven me to this and now . . . I understand why you wanted vengeance for Edward because he was my brother, remember? It seemed right at first, but now . . ."

He realized he had not reached her. Her face had softened, her eyes grew dreamy. "It will make Edward happy."

"My God! Edward happy!" He made a last appeal, hands extended. "Inez, Edward is *dead!* He's a ghost if he's anything at all. What about me?"

She pulled her mind back to the present, the room, and Ewing. She picked up her sewing. "You? You really never mattered. I really died when—Edward did."

XVII

There was another mound in the desert cemetery and the man who had sought to flee from death was now eternally embraced in it. The town turned out in a body and Vic Hayes was a sorrow on men's tongues. But the forgetful busyness of life's rhythm resumed as the mourners dispersed.

Three men accompanied the Burruds to their house. Wayne drove Abbie home, then turned the buggy and returned to the Burruds himself. They waited for him in the big main room. Once again, Frank stood before the fireplace, hands clasped behind his back. He had aged badly and his face looked acid grooved, his eyes haggard.

His voice was heavy, slow. "Vic Hayes is gone. That leaves Jesse . . . Joel . . . Hal . . . Lew . . . Wayne . . . me. Here we are—what's left. But what about tomorrow? Or next week? Five of us? Four? Who?"

There was nothing to say. Wayne broke the silence. "You've got something in mind, Frank?"

The older man pursed his lips, face clouded. He took a breath, expelled it. "When this thing started, we knew what we faced. We figured we could protect one another—or be ready for any kind of trouble. That won't work. Vic wanted to leave—just pull out and go. I was against it, but today we know Vic was right. I was wrong. If we stay here, we die—one by one. Leaving's the only sensible thing to do."

Hal Grayson shot a troubled look at Wayne and then down at the floor. Lew Kearney frowned at his folded hands. Joel Ramsey scratched his head and then smoothed his cowlick.

Wayne said, "I think we'd be giving up just before we won. Maybe we're adding everything up on the bad side. I think we're a lot closer to the killer than we ever were."

Jesse put in, "I'd like to believe that."

Wayne answered. "Look at it. He got Vic, and that's the thing that sticks high in our minds. But he's made mistakes and he's left sign. He's failed twice to get me. Hal had a glimpse of him. Vance found that Indian bow and that might be pretty important."

"He'll lay low."

"Can he? He's put pressure on us, made us jump at shadows. But how do we know what pressure we've put on him? He knows six of us were looking for him. There's the law, too. He must feel like a fox with two packs of hounds closing in."

Frank said slowly, "I wish we *were* closing in."

Lew Kearney slapped his hand on his leg. "I think Wayne's right. I never looked at it just that way, but it makes sense. Besides, I want to stay here myself. When a man's found a girl that—"

His face tightened in determination. “I’ll back Wayne. Besides, Ewing Vance is doing a hell of a lot more than Hank Malloy.”

The men covertly looked at one another and each searched his own mind. Frank thoughtfully rubbed the back of his neck. “That’s the way you’ll have it then?”

Joel nodded, moon face serious. “I got a good job and I reckon I can have it as long as I want. Ewing ain’t a bad boss. I like it here.”

Frank swung to Grayson. “Hal?”

“I—don’t reckon I can leave. I’m beginning to get somewhere with my business.”

Frank looked around at Jesse, who said quickly, “Whatever you think, Frank.”

The older brother surrendered. “I guess we can stick together a while longer. Maybe I lost my nerve after burying Vic. I’m mighty thankful that all of you gave it back to me.”

The meeting broke up. Abbie waited for Wayne behind the barred door and bolted shutters. He gave his little knock and she admitted him. He told her what had happened and of Frank’s discouragement. That surprised her. “Then we’re leaving?”

“Maybe I’m risking too much, but we’re sticking. Lew Kearney backed me and I guess that’s what decided it.”

Abbie kissed him. “That’s what I wanted—to stay. I like this country and this house. Sometimes

I've looked around at the things that are ours and I know I couldn't bring myself to leave them. I don't want to be driven out and yet I'm scared—about you. Nothing's worth while if you're not here to share it."

"I'll be here."

"I'm sure of it. It has to be that way. Surely, the killer is bound to slip. He's had too much luck, and luck changes. It's time now."

Wayne laughed, put his arms around her and swung her to the table. He blew out the lamp and, still holding her, guided her to the bedroom. He kissed her. "Luck—and time. They're both working for us."

He could not find sleep immediately. Luck and hope—was that all he could depend upon? Was there something overlooked? A simple little thing so obvious they had passed it by?

He doggedly set himself to review every death. Bedford Drumbo killed in town. Skip Adams murdered in his own house. Vic Hayes killed miles to the south. Still, the bushwhacker could have made a huge circle back to town. Someone in town who had been at Lawrence—always this combination of facts but nothing more. Not a person he knew had been in Kansas.

How about the try to kill him, the burning of the Burrud barn and the note that was so boldly put upon his door? Close to town again. But the bushwhack on the road was some distance away. Yet Wayne had been left afoot when the horses were killed. He wondered if Vance had met anyone in a hurry on the desert road that day. He'd ask the law man tomorrow. A mighty thin and hopeless thing, but nothing should be overlooked. He drifted off to sleep.

Just after noon, he pulled in at the marshal's office. Ewing Vance sat behind his desk facing a far wall that held reward dodgers. Ewing's thoughts were far away and none too pleasant. Wayne cleared his throat and Vance started, swung around, peering against the bright sunlight behind Wayne.

"Oh, it's you, Nelson. Something on your mind?"

"Several things. You never did say where you found that bow."

"That! Wayne, like I said, how could I tell you exactly where I found it? I'll show you, next time I'm out. Main thing is, I found it."

"I still can't figure how we passed it up."

"Now if that's all." Vance opened a desk drawer, I'm pretty busy—"

"Not all."

"More trouble?"

"No—another question. Remember that time I was bushwhacked?"

"Sure. I did all I could. Followed trail until it faded out."

"I know, I can't remember when I was so glad

to see someone as when you came along. But did you see anyone along the road that morning—before you met me?"

"Who would I see?"

"I think whoever tried for me cut back to the road—like whoever killed Vic Hayes. Grayson glimpsed him real close to the road."

"What's Vic Hayes got to do with you?"

"Some sort of thing, Vance. You can see that. Now if you met someone miles away from that canyon, you wouldn't think much of it at the time. I thought you might have. It could have been someone both of us know real well. It'd almost have to be. Bed, Skip, and Vic were killed by someone right here in Florence. I figure it was the same man who tried for me."

Vance eased back in his chair. "Wish I could go along with that, Wayne. But I didn't see anyone. Vic Hayes was killed by someone who wanted the bullion on the stage. Two different things."

Wayne considered this. He finally slapped his hands down on the chair arms and pushed himself up. "Maybe you're right. Just don't seem to make sense that way. But you'd know best."

He left. Vance sat unmoving, body clammy and throat dry. Guesses, he told himself, nothing but guesses. He passed his hand over his forehead, discovering it, too, was moist. He let his breath out in a quivering sigh as he realized that one wrong word or act might turn full-blown suspicion to him. Fortunately, all of them still looked to the star on his chest. But for how long? This was thin ice now, so leave things alone no matter what Inez thought or demanded.

He left the office, reluctantly holding his pace to that of a casual stroller. He gave Joel, behind the bar, a brief wave of the hand and crossed the saloon to his own quarters. Inez, in the kitchen, looked up from over a dough board. He dropped his hat on the table and thudded into one of the chairs. Inez asked in a faint contempt that stung Vance, "What now?"

"Wayne Nelson's snooping and guessing."

"Let him."

"Leave that damn dough alone and listen to me!" He spoke more calmly when she turned, wiping her floured hands on her apron. "It's more than guess, Inez. Nelson is getting answers, at least in his own mind. Thank God, he's still coming to me!"

"You know what to do. I told you he'd have to be next."

"You don't understand. If Nelson is getting close, so are the others. What he thinks, you can bet the others think. We have to let things slide—do nothing."

"No!"

"It can't be any other way. Inez, we've got three of them."

She came to the table and spaced each word

carefully. "I won't be satisfied until all of them are gone. Understand that! We won't stop now."

His fist banged down on the table. "We will! We have to!"

They faced each other in a silent battle. Then she slowly turned and went back to the dough board. Vance sat down again as she started kneading once more. Then she spoke without turning her head. "You won't do anything more?"

"Not for a while, at least. Maybe not at all. I'm sick of this whole business."

"Then I will. Edward deserves no less. If you won't, I will."

Anger flooded through him. He jumped up, circled the table and grabbed her shoulders, swinging her around. "You'll do nothing—understand!"

Her eyes locked with his in a steady, calm gaze. "You've turned to jelly. You're afraid. I'm not."

"Afraid! You know better, Inez."

She slowly disengaged his hands from her shoulders. The act in itself was scathing, contemptuous. "Then do your duty to Edward—and me."

She turned back to the dough. "I see Edward lying in his own blood. That's all I ever see. I know that if you won't finish this thing, I will."

"Inez, are you blood crazy!"

She calmly considered, head held to one side.

"No, I don't think so. I only want things set right for Edward after all these years. See to it."

He was suddenly frightened of her but she should not know it. He tried to hold his voice steady. "Let's think it over, Inez. I mean," he added hastily as he saw her anger, "we have to figure out how to go about it. We don't want to get caught, do we? Then the others would go free."

She relaxed against the table. "You're right. We have to figure out some way."

He edged toward the door. "You think about it and so will I. I have to get down the street now. We'll talk about it later."

He was out the door, standing in the bright sun. It was hot but he felt a chill along his spine. He didn't know where he walked, didn't care. He was only aware of the quiver of his nerves. He strode blindly along the street and then, instinctively, cut away lest someone see and stop him.

The woman was mad! She must always have been since that horrible morning in Lawrence. She had gone into shock, he had known that, but it must have gone deeper. The coming of the nine had released it—like an explosion. Now she was filled with blood lust, a vengeance mania.

His had been the delusion that a man might seek his own justice, but *that* was not insanity. Where would this lead? He couldn't stop her.

Nor did he dare stop now himself. Inez would act and both of them would be discovered. He was trapped. He could hold off a little while under the pretext of planning the next kill, but only for a limited time. Maybe there was some way he could get Inez out of here. His mind fastened on the thought and a certain sanity returned.

He realized he had walked out beyond the edge of town. He needed some place where he could think. He turned back, stopped. He didn't want to go home, nor to the marshal's office. His eyes caught the squat, rambling adobe of Madam Verona's. This time of day there'd be only the girls and they'd probably be up in their rooms, resting in preparation for the night.

He could always do pretty much as he pleased at Madam Verona's; talk with the Madam herself in a lazy, friendly way, or drink at the bar with the girls or alone at a table. He needed something like that now.

The Negro maid admitted him. The main room was empty and he refused the woman's offer to call one of the girls or Madam. She asked no questions when he indicated a table and went to the bar, picked a bottle and glass. "Nothin' else, Mistuh Vance?"

"Nothing."

She padded away, leaving him alone in the ornate parlor. He poured a stiff drink, downed it and eased back in his chair, waiting for the whiskey bite, feeling as though he had escaped from his pressures and problems. He hadn't, of course, but he would think about them as soon as his nerves returned to their sheaths and the liquor had dispelled the inward chill Inez caused. Leave town—that was the answer. Maybe he could work up some reason to go to San Francisco, leave Joel to run the bar.

He felt warm now and the reaction to his turmoil gave him a feeling of physical lassitude. Don't think for a few moments, he told himself, just *be,* until a measure of balance returns. Then think this thing out. But he didn't think so much as let his emotions carry his brain along. His horror of the depths Inez had revealed strengthened his panic. He sought a motive for leaving that would not fool her.

He poured another drink. The fog of fear began to dissipate. Joel could handle the bar and he could tell Inez that he planned to remodel the Gila. He and Inez would go to San Francisco to buy a new bar, new furniture, maybe some paintings.

Fern Eccles appeared in the doorway. Her pretty, vapid face lighted. He wasn't aware of her until she stood beside him, plump arm dropping on his shoulder, her blue eyes dancing. "Ewing! You come to see Fern?"

He flinched away, then hid his irritation. He gave her a slap that stung through her dress, grinned and shook his head. “Not this time. But have a drink.”

She winced at his slap but smiled, pulled out a chair and sat down. He poured the drink, knowing this would be the quickest way to be rid of her. She’d chatter, try to interest him and, that failing, she’d leave.

She aimlessly touched her high-piled blonde hair as she talked, smiled and moved about so that her breasts quivered under her thin dress. Her chatter was meaningless as the babble of a brook—a woman built to please a man, uncomplicated, no dark undercurrents, no madness. Inez’ brooding eyes appeared between him and Fern and the illusion startled him out of his thoughts.

There was only Fern, the empty doll. His ears caught her words in the middle of a sentence. A cold shock went through him. “What did you say?”

“Ewing, you ain’t been listening! I said it was funny about that bow.”

“What bow?”

“Why, that Injun bow you found.”

He forced himself to keep his voice light. “What about it? What’s so funny?”

“You finding it. I got to thinking how you used to tell me about arrows ’n bows and things.”

He felt something slowly coil about his chest. “Me?”

"Why, sure. Remember once we got to talking about how good a shot you are with rifles, Colts 'n almost everything, even Injun arrows. I didn't believe it about the arrows but you said you could always hit dead-center bullseye with one. You said you had a bow or used to have one."

Vance felt his mouth and throat go dry. "I haven't used a bow for years. Left the one I had back in Kentucky. How about another drink, Fern?"

"Oughtn't—but I will."

He poured, marveling that he kept his hand steady. He filled his own glass, speaking carelessly. "Have you mentioned this to anyone?"

"Clean forgot it . . . until just now. Don't know why it popped into my head after all this time."

"Happens that way. Forget it. It doesn't mean anything and I must've been drunk." He lifted his glass. "Our healths, Fern."

"Sure, Ewing. Long life to both of us and lots of fun."

She smiled coyly over the glass and downed the liquor. Ewing also drank. But the liquid fire could not erase his cold, sick sensation. He knew what he must do.

Murder had followed him here.

XVIII

When Wayne left the marshal's office, he walked slowly down the street, wondering why he felt he had just missed something; that a word, a question, a subtle action on his part might have made the difference. Perhaps, unknowingly, he had built up too much hope—or maybe it was something about Vance. Come to think of it, Ewing hadn't been at ease during the whole time, as though he had been suspicious, alert, on guard. Why?

Wayne had no satisfactory answer by the time he turned into the general store. There were but few customers, among them Lorain Tryon at the dry-goods counter. The girl smiled and it struck him again that she was really a beautiful girl. No wonder Lew Kearney still hoped for her.

She said, "I never had a chance to tell you how sorry I am Dad let you go. . . ."

He laughed. "Why, maybe it was a favor! I'm going to work my farm, like I would have done long ago."

"I'm glad." Her voice grew wistful. "I wish I had a place of my own—like you and Abbie."

"It will come. You and Lew—"

"I don't see him anymore. He just never—tries to see me like he used to. I guess he's found someone around the mines. I hear there are some pretty girls up there."

"I never saw any that could come near you. There's something troubling Lew. It's no other girl, I can tell you that. It will pass."

"What is it? Maybe if I knew, I could help."

He hesitated, bit at his lip. "It's something he wants to get cleared up. He will tell you when the right time comes. Maybe soon now. Don't worry. Lew doesn't think about any other girl but you."

He hastily left the store to avoid further questions and went to the Gila Saloon. Joel yawned over the bar but he came to life when Wayne entered. The door to the living quarters was closed, and there was no sign of the Vances.

Joel deftly filled a glass. "Glad you come. Sure been dull around here the last hour."

Joel was in a mood to talk about Vic Hayes. "I still get shivers when I think about Vic. I wonder who's going to be next? Ewing is working hard on it. I sure hope he finds that killer."

"Think he will?"

"Vance is a mighty persistent man."

Wayne leaned against the bar. "What's he like, Joel?"

Joel considered the question. "Well, it's hard to say. I like Ewing, but him and Inez are a strange pair."

"But Vance seems to be all right. A little pushy, maybe."

“I don’t know—something about ’em. I’ve never heard her laugh and the few times she smiles, you’d swear it hurt her. . . . Sometimes, I think there’s something riding both of them with spurs. She’ll look at Ewing as though she’d be glad to stick a knife in him. Again, she’ll get excited like she’s had good news. Mostly, though, she acts like she died a long time ago and is just walking around out of habit. Real funny, them two, especially her.”

Wayne turned the information over in his mind, wondering how Inez looked when she was excited. Then he wondered what caused it and asked Joel.

“No idea. She just gets that way sometimes. Last time was when they brought Vic in. Course, the whole town was upset then so maybe it wasn’t unusual.”

“No other time?”

“Well, the time Skip was murdered she hung around a lot—listening, mostly. Funny woman. Sometimes she acts like she enjoyed trouble.”

“Is Vance that way?”

“No. He’s mighty busy now between here and the marshal’s job. He wants to run both jobs, even though he’s said himself I can handle the bar. But he gets real wound up.”

“Wearing the badge is no easy job.”

“That’s hellfire sure after all that’s happened here! I think it’s getting under Vance’s skin that he can't get anywhere. Sometimes he acts like he's scared it'll beat him. But he rides out and tries. You can hand him that."

Joel glanced at the far door. "Like this morning, he went down to the jail office—then come back here. You can hear voices through them walls though you can't make out the words. He was in there. Him 'n her and some sort of argument. Then he tore out."

Wayne finished his drink. It was interesting enough, but it was not important. Inez would not be easy to get along with. Wayne dropped a coin on the bar and turned away. A thought jumped into his mind. "Ever heard them mention Kansas?"

"They're from Kentucky. Nary a word about Kansas unless . . ."

"Unless?"

"One time Inez asked a whole bunch of questions about the nine of us. Wanted to know where we come from, where we'd been." He smiled crookedly. "She sure had me sweating for a time. Real interested, but, hell, it was just plain prying. About all you could say for it."

Wayne leaned against the bar, eyes afar as he tried to find some meaning to this. There wasn't any, but still he had that same strange sense that he had missed something subtle and yet obvious. He turned back to the batwings. "Got to get along."

Joel hurried around the bar and caught up with him as Wayne pushed open the batwings. They stood under the wooden canopy and looked down the somnolent street. The sun's brightness made them squint. Joel sighed, "Sure dead today."

Wayne noticed Joel's white apron, missed the telltale bulge of a holster beneath it. "Joel, you're not wearing a gun!"

"Don't have to wear one. I keep one close to hand under the bar. I always leave it there because it's Ewing's—the bar gun. I got another at home where I can reach it in a minute."

"But between times!"

"Now, I'm either at the saloon or home. No one's going to jump me right on the main street. If I go some place like the Burruds', I wear the one I keep at home."

"You're not safe anywhere, Joel. You know that."

"I walk two blocks to work and two home. More'n half the time it's in daylight—when Vance takes over the bar at night. No one'd dare take a shot at me!"

Wayne shrugged, walked off to the general store. He bought farm tools and a bright brooch for Abbie, then drove home, shoulders hunched against the sun.

Early the next morning, Wayne started to work over at the north fence before Abbie called him to breakfast. They discussed the first crop they would put in. Abbie suddenly lifted her head. "Someone's coming—in a hurry."

Wayne heard a horse coming, fast. He darted to a far corner and grabbed the rifle, jacked a shell in the chamber as he strode to the door. Horse and rider thundered into the yard. Lew Kearney swung out of the saddle as Wayne jumped into the yard to meet him.

"Joel!" Lew said. "He's in jail! I stopped to tell the Burruds then come on here. I figured we all ought to know it and—"

"Hold up, Lew. Make sense! Joel's in jail? When, and what for?"

"This morning. Vance arrested him. For murder!"

Wayne caught his breath. "Murder! Joel Ramsey?" A new fear clutched at him. "Who's dead? One of us?"

"No. It was Fern Eccles, one of Madam Verona's girls. Someone waited last night until she was, 'scuse me, Abbie, alone in her room and he shot her. Warm nights like these, the windows are open. He fired from outside. The bullet caught her dead center in the heart."

Abbie demanded, "And it was Joel?"

Wayne said flatly, "I don't believe it."

"They sent for Ewing. Killer was gone by then, of course. They didn't find nothing. But this morning Vance went back and found a gun, one shot fired. They figure the killer dropped it when he run. It was Joel's gun. Vance says this killing's a lot like Vic's and just as senseless as his and Skip's and Bed's."

"Joel kill them?" Wayne glared at Lew. "Damn it! no one can believe a thing like that!"

"Vance figures there was some sort of trouble and—"

"Hogwash! How about this girl—this Fern?"

"Joel swears he never left his place last night, but he can't prove it. But he admits the gun is his." Lew glanced at Abbie, blushed. "Joel's gone to Madam Verona's a few times. Vance figures something went wrong between him and this girl. Anyway, he shot her."

Abbie cut in. "But if he didn't leave his house?"

Lew sighed. "Whole point is, he could've. It's no distance from where he lives to the Madam's."

"Have you seen Joel?" Wayne asked.

"No, but some men went with Vance to arrest him and I got it from them. Vance won't let anyone talk to Joel. When I got the news, I told Hal Grayson and then came tearing out here."

Wayne thought, Ewing Vance has made a bad mistake. Joel simply couldn't have done this thing. Circumstantial evidence and no more. Joel had no proof he had remained at home and the gun was damning . . . the gun! Wayne recalled his talk with Joel just yesterday.

Abbie caught his sudden start. "Wayne, you know something about this?"

"I just remembered. Lew, can we get into Joel's house?"

"No one locks a door and Joel sure hasn't anything a person'd want to steal."

"Let's get to town. If I can prove something Joel told me—Come on, Lew. Might be we can get Joel out of jail."

They wasted no time in getting to town and they had merely to open Joel's door and step into his little adobe shack at the far end of the main street. At first glance, there was no sign of a gun and Wayne's hopes dropped in a sickening lurch. But he looked carefully about the room. Joel had a gun here for his own protection. Where would a man keep it close to hand?

He then saw a cubbyhole of a room holding a brass bedstead. Wayne strode to it and lifted the pillow, felt under the blanket. Nothing. He ran his hands under the mattress. His fingers struck metal and he pulled out a heavy revolver. Lew looked at it and then at Wayne, surprised and puzzled. Wayne checked the loads. The weapon had not been fired. He looked up at Lew. "When did Joel work at the Gila yesterday?"

"Most of the day to right after supper time. Then he came home, or said he did."

"This girl at Madam's—what time was she shot?"

"They say around eleven last night."

Wayne nodded, eyes distant. "The Gila'd still be open. Joel couldn't return to the Gila, take a gun from under the bar and leave without being seen. Not a chance in the world!"

"What're you getting at?"

Wayne pushed the weapon in his waistband. "Joel swears he didn't leave here. He's telling the truth, Lew. Someone wants him to hang for murdering that girl and I think it's the killer."

Lew's jaw dropped. Wayne's eyes grew cold. "But our killer has made a bad mistake . . . maybe the big one. Let's go to Madam Verona's."

XIX

It was not far from Joel's to Madam Verona's, though they were on opposite sides of the town and it would be easy, Wayne realized, to go there without being seen. Madam's place had a withdrawn and barricaded look but repeated knockings brought a Negro maid to the door. "There ain't nothing here today, Gen'men. We've had trouble."

Wayne said, "I have to talk with Madam Verona."

"She won't see nobody!"

Wayne blocked her attempt to close the door. "Tell her she might save a life."

The woman hesitated. "I see. You wait."

The minutes dragged. The door reopened and the maid motioned them in. The sunlight, filtered through lowered blinds, was not kind to the dusty drapes or the rug on the floor. Wayne caught the dull gleam of a small bar in the corner, noted the ornate carvings on chairs and sofas, the gaudy, ruffled pillows that adorned them.

Madam Verona entered. She looked weary, pouches formed under her eyes and the rice powder could not conceal weary facial lines. Madam gave Wayne a swift, sure appraisal.

Her eyes turned briefly to Lew and then back to Wayne, sensing that he was the important one. She sat down on a sofa, erect and prim as a dowager. "We're not looking for company today, Mister—what with poor Fern dead. And we don't want gawpers. If you've pulled a trick just to satisfy—"

"I haven't."

Unconvinced, she waved them the seats. She toyed with her string of pearls. "What's this about saving a life? Whose life?"

"Joel Ramsey's."

"Him! But he killed Fern."

"That's what they say. But do you believe it? I don't."

She studied him for a long moment. "Any proof?"

"That's why I'm here. I want to find out."

Madam Verona called the maid and ordered drinks. When they were served, she asked, "Now, what's this about?"

Wayne asked, "Did Joel often come here?"

"Enough that we knew him. Fern was kind of his special friend, too. Can't understand why he shot—"

"I don't think he did. He wasn't here last night?"

"No. But he must have been just outside, waiting a time she was alone in her room. I just can't understand it! Everyone of us liked Joel. He was always laughing or joking, playing the guitar and singing."

"Then he and Fern never quarreled?"

Madam Verona finished her drink. "Never. Why, just yesterday, Fern was saying he was always nice to her and she liked him."

"Then why should he shoot her?"

"You never can tell much about a person. Maybe Joel got jealous of the other men. I've seen that happen. Maybe he's been a killer all along, kind of hidden deep. Something Fern did or said tripped it off. I've seen that happen, too."

Wayne felt defeated. There was nothing here, but he questioned her further and she patiently answered him. But for all his probing, he learned nothing new.

Finally, Madam Verona arose to end the meeting. She went with him and Lew to the door. She put her hand on his arm. "Joel's your friend and you're sticking by him. Damn few would do that. But it's no use. He killed her."

She sighed and dropped her hand. "Fern was such a good girl, too! Everyone liked her. Just yesterday Vance dropped in. He had a drink and a talk with her."

"Vance?"

Madam Verona's eyes veiled. "He's marshal, so he has to drop in now and then. Got along with all of us, especially Fern. You can see how well-liked she was, bless her soul!"

She opened the door. Wayne thanked her and left. He adjusted his hat brim against the sun and slowly walked away with Lew. Something about the interview nagged and worried him. He couldn't pin it down as he trudged back to the town.

At the Gila Saloon several men stood at the bar, listening raptly to Ewing Vance. Wayne saw Hal Grayson at the far end and edged in beside him. Vance paused in serving his customers and shook his head worriedly at a question. "I'll have to get someone here. Can't hold two jobs, that's sure, and my wife only helps when she has to. Best that way. A bar's no place for a woman."

Someone said, "You shouldn't have arrested Joel."

"I sure don't want to. But there was his gun laying right outside that window. Of course he denied it, but you can figure it out for yourselves. He could easy get from his place to Madam Verona's and back again in ten or fifteen minutes. He'd never be seen, late as it was. His gun had been fired. What else could I do? I sure hope he can find witnesses to back up his story. But if he killed that girl, then he should hang! That's only justice."

Wayne twisted away from the bar, heading toward one of the tables. He glimpsed Inez watching and listening through the crack of her door but she quickly closed it. He sat down at a table. He paid no attention to the steady rumble of Vance's voice. The men listened like ghouls, Wayne thought. For that matter, so had Inez but a moment ago.

His mind fastened suddenly on the talk he and Joel had about Ewing and Inez. Acting strange, Joel had said, nervous and excited, and Inez had pried at Joel about the past of the nine who had come to town.

A thought that he had often considered suddenly combined with what Joel had said. Every killing and every attempt had been made close to town. And then that Indian bow Vance had found where Wayne knew all of them had searched before—strange it had come up *after* they had told Vance they suspected a fire-arrow. How did it happen that all trails Vance followed vanished into nowhere?

He heard Vance speaking again. "I knew that gun. Joel kept it with him all the time. Used to put it here under the bar when he came to work."

But he didn't! Wayne sat electrified. If Joel had gone directly from his home, he would have used the weapon resting right now in Wayne's waistband. It was unfired.

Vance must be lying. But it would take a lot of proof to break that assurance if this fantastic idea was true. Wayne suddenly thought of the tension and fear in which they had lived for so long. He recalled his own statement that the tension must be equally great on the killer.

He checked his eagerness as he walked casually to the bar. He tugged at Grayson's sleeve. "Hal, see you outside?"

Grayson gave him a puzzled look but followed Wayne out of the saloon and down the street for several yards. Wayne made sure no one was in earshot. "Hal, can you bring Frank and Jesse here?"

"What's up?"

"We're going to get Joel out of jail."

"Try to break him out? We won't have a chance!"

"No—but try to put the real killer in there in his place."

"Who!"

"I'll tell you when you bring the Burruds—and I'll get Lew. Your place open? Good. We'll meet there. Kind of drift out of town and ease back in with the Burruds in case someone's watching."

Something in Wayne's intensity made Grayson keep questions to himself. "I reckon you know what you're doing."

Wayne returned to the Gila, pulled Lew away from the bar and soon they waited for the others in Grayson's quarters. Wayne promised to answer Lew's questions when the others arrived. He paced restlessly, checking over the sequence of events and always arriving at the same solution.

Grayson and the Burruds arrived, eager, curious and puzzled. Wayne told them of his line of reasoning and the conclusion to which it led. Gradually he swung them around, not to firm belief, but to an acknowledgment that he just might be right.

Frank asked, “But how do you prove it?”

“There’s the nub. Vance won’t be one to admit anything. But he’s had some close calls. He can’t be too sure of how much we know. We’ll make him show himself.”

“How?”

Wayne told his plan. Grayson, looking a little frightened at the part he was to play, shook his head. “I don’t think it will work.”

“We won’t know until we try. If it’s not Vance, then maybe it will flush the real killer. What can we lose? If Vance is innocent, he won’t fall into the trap. If he is . . .”

Frank frowned then looked up. “All right. Like you say, we can lose nothing.”

Wayne and Grayson returned to the Gila, Wayne showing more confidence than he felt. There were still a few loiterers at the bar. Wayne and Grayson ordered, loafed over their drinks until at last they were alone with Vance. Wayne nudged Grayson.

Hal took a drink, ordered another. He spoke a little loudly. “Don’t know why, but this killing business makes me think of Vic Hayes. Something about that fellow I saw keeps bothering me."

Vance poured a refill. "What about him?"

"Keeps just beyond me. But I swear I've seen that one before. Something in the shape of him."

"You were pretty far," Vance said dryly. "At least, by your story."

Hal said nothing more. Vance went to the far end of the bar to clean glasses. Hal stared hard at Vance. Vance didn't notice it at first but then he glanced at Grayson and away. Shortly, his eyes came back. Grayson still stared, brows knotted. The marshal concentrated on the glasses but he threw covert, increasingly nervous glances at Grayson.

Wayne appeared to notice his companion's stare. "Hey, Hal! What's wrong with you?"

Grayson's voice was a hoarse whisper. "No! It can't be!"

Wayne caught Vance's sudden start. "What can't be, Hal?"

Grayson stared at Vance. "Same size—same build."

Vance strode up. "What's wrong with you?"

"Nothing—nothing, Vance. Wayne, come with me. I want to look at a horse."

"Hey! Wait!" Vance called but the two of them hurried out.

Outside, Grayson asked, "Did I act all right?"

"Nothing wrong with you. We'll have to see how it worked."

They turned a corner and then retraced their way along the alley back to the rear of the Gila. They saw the stable where Vance kept his horse, the windows and door of the living quarters in the building. Wayne said, "If he's scared, he'll be watching. Act like we're trying to get a look at his horse. If we see him, we'll back off—fast."

They drifted toward the stable. The house door opened and Vance appeared. Wayne wheeled away, Grayson following at his heels. They whipped out of sight around a corner. There was no pursuit, suspicious in itself. They halted and Grayson looked at Wayne. "By God, it's working!"

"I think so. You know what to do now, Hal? Make the round of the stores—Canby's, the blacksmith shop. Act nervous and ask all kinds of questions about Vance. Ask what he was doing last night during the time Inez tended bar to relieve him. Then head for your place and wait."

He gave Grayson several minutes and then he strolled back to the Gila. Vance had returned to the bar but he stood quite still when Wayne entered. His flecked green eyes were sharp and his face more pale than usual. "What's wrong with you and Grayson?"

Wayne looked embarrassed. "Nothing, Ewing, except Hal had me all mixed up. Got me outside and said he wanted to look at your horse. Then he took off like a scared Indian when he saw you. I think he's crazy as a June bug. Says he thinks he knows who shot Vic Hayes."

"Why'd he want to look at my horse?"

"That's what I asked him, but he said he had to think it over real good and ask a few questions before he went to the mayor."

"The mayor! But I'm the law!"

"Hal said he wouldn't talk to you. That's when I figured he was crazy or drunk."

Vance studied him. Then he pretended to dismiss it, gave Wayne his drink. Wayne watched Vance do meaningless tasks with an increasing nervousness. Finally Vance jerked off his apron and strode to the far door, called, "Inez! Can you handle the place a while? I got to check on Joel Ramsey at the jail."

Inez appeared and Vance, with a curt nod to Wayne, hurried out. Inez stood for a long time in the doorway, her brooding eyes remaining on the emptily swinging batwings. Wayne studied his drink. All had worked well so far. Vance would trail Hal and the further he went, the more his danger would seem to mount.

Inez came to the bar. Wayne met her dark look, then she turned her back. Silence came in the big room and Wayne could hear the loud ticking of the clock all too clearly.

Boots thudded on the outer porch and a group

of teamsters from Canby's station streamed in. Inez served them. Wayne eased out of the press and strolled outside. He shot a swift look around, did not see Vance. He moved fast then to the corner of the building, down its length to the rear.

He paused at the corner. No one was in sight. He walked to the rear door, grasped the knob and turned it, steadily. It was locked and he whispered an oath, tested the nearby window. It lifted easily and silently. He lifted himself to the sill, clambered inside. He could hear, muted by the walls, the noise the teamsters made in the outer bar. Inez would be busy enough and Vance would be combing the town for Grayson.

Wayne looked briefly around the kitchen, certain there would be nothing here. He moved into the small living room and now could hear the bar noise more clearly. He sought a Bible that might have the family record, a marriage certificate, a letter—anything that might place the Vances in Kansas.

The center table was bare except for a pile of knitting. The walls held some steel prints. There was no secretary, desk or bookcase, only a sideboard with a single bottle of whiskey. He catfooted across the room and opened the drawers. Silverware, odds and ends, nothing of value.

He felt time slipping away as he stepped back, eyes casting about. The door to the bedroom stood open. He listened to the bar sounds, gained fresh courage from them, and entered the bedroom. It was as plain and as empty of significance as the room he had just quitted.

Then he saw the picture on the dresser. Ewing, he thought at first, but his eyes swung back to it. A Yankee uniform? He snatched up the frame, staring at the face that calmly looked back at him.

It was Yankee. He recognized the insignia—chaplain. This man had Ewing's thin lips and the same skin pallor. There were other startling resemblances. Wayne worked the picture out of the frame. He read the bold, black writing.

"To my beloved wife, Inez—Edward Vance, Lawrence, Kansas—May, 1863."

Wayne's fingers tightened on the picture. Edward Vance—it could only be Ewing's brother—and Inez had been his wife. In Lawrence!

A burst of noise from the bar made him hastily shove the picture inside his shirt and hurry through the kitchen and outside. He strode away, wings on his feet.

He had the connection . . . the proof! Everything fitted as neatly as a whipstock in a socket. His suspect could easily have done every killing, made every move. He didn't know why Fern Eccles had been killed, but Joel Ramsey had been scheduled to swing for it.

Ewing Vance was the killer—and he wore a law badge!

Wayne did not forget that Vance would be following Grayson's erratic trail from place to place, so he moved swiftly but cautiously. As he came to Grayson's home, the Burruds and Lew stepped from hiding places across the street. Wayne signaled them to come on and opened the door. Grayson wheeled from the table, hand at his holstered gun. Relief showed in his face. "It's you. Did you find anything?"

Frank, Jesse and Lew came in, closing the door after them. Wayne pulled out the photograph and placed it on the table. They looked at it, read the inscription.

Frank Burrud's soft sigh broke the silence. "So that's it. Vengeance, like we thought from the beginning. Once you get something like this, you can see how Vance could have done every murder. What a hell of a thing."

"Inez and Ewing," Jesse said in awed wonder. "One driving on the other . . . But what about Fern Eccles?"

Frank said, "We'll find out. Main thing is, what do we do now?"

They looked to Wayne. He noted that each wore belt and gun as had become their habit. He spoke slowly. "Up to now, Vance has picked his own place and time. Now it's our turn, right here. We've forced Vance to move. He doesn't know about this picture yet, but he figures Hal is close to identifying Vic's killer. He's worried and uncertain. But he figures Hal hasn't talked yet. He has to shut you up before you do."

"My God!" Grayson breathed.

"We'll force him to come here. You know what he's like. This'll be a showdown but we've wanted it. Better get back to your places. I'll stay with Hal."

Lew asked, "We stop him outside?"

"No. Let him come in, then follow—fast."

Wayne picked up the photograph and the three men filed out. Grayson mopped at his face. "I'm the bait in the trap. It's a funny feeling."

"Over soon, Hal—all over."

Hal sat down at the table and poured a drink with a slight tremble of his hand. But he checked the loads in his gun before he downed the whiskey in a single gulp. Wayne refused the drink Hal offered.

Wait. An illusion, perhaps, but all the usual sounds of the town died away into a breathless suspense. Vance moved along a path that would inevitably lead to this room—like Death, slowly, implacably coming. But whose death?

Grayson felt the nightmare quality. "When in the hell is he coming!"

"Get hold of yourself, Hal. You got to act like you're scared."

"I don't have to act. I *am* scared."

The oppressive silence resumed. Both of them jumped when a light knock sounded on the door. Wayne, with a fierce gesture to Hal, stepped into the kitchen. The knock sounded again, sharp and peremptory. Grayson slowly crossed the room and opened the door.

Ewing's voice sounded easy and friendly. "Hoped you'd be home, Hal. I been aiming to talk to you."

Grayson's voice sounded choked. "Talk? About what?"

"A lot of things. Can't I come in, Hal?"

He did not wait for a reply. The door closed and Vance spoke again. "Something's bothering you about that stage hold-up. It bothers me, too. I'd like to get it cleared up. If you've got any information, you ought to give it to me."

They were well into the room. Wayne touched his gun in the holster, felt a tightening in his chest as he stepped out. They stood by the table, Grayson as if hypnotized. Vance smiled but the green eyes were ice cold and piercing. Light from the window made a mocking glitter of the badge on his shirt.

His head jerked around when Wayne appeared. His jaw hung slack and then his thin lips moved in a smile. "Didn't know you had company, Hal. We'll talk later."

He turned to the door just as it opened. Frank and Jesse pushed in, Lew behind them. Vance stepped back to the table. Lew closed the door and stood against it. Vance looked from one grim face to the other. His pallor increased and his eyes flicked about the room. He spoke arrogantly. "This begins to look like a big meeting. I'd better leave."

Wayne said evenly, "You'll stay, Vance."

Vance swung around. "Why?"

Wayne placed the photograph on the table. Vance looked at the picture. His eyes widened in horrified amazement and his hand clenched. At last he looked up at Wayne, flecked eyes hard as green pebbles. The angles of his face grew more pronounced, the planes of his cheeks longer. He seemed to ask a wordless question.

Wayne nodded. "We know. Bed Drumbo, Skip Adams, Vic Hayes—murdered. None of them had a chance. Two tries at me. You burned the Burrud barn with a fire arrow. Now Fern Eccles is murdered and you put the blame on Joel Ramsey. You figured to do the hanging after the law had sentenced him—another Quantrell man killed. My God, Vance! Have you gone blood mad!"

Vance jerked as though Wayne had slapped him. His eyes wavered down to the picture. "My brother—Quantrell's men killed him. They shot me down in the street. Inez has never been the same since. Then you came and I remembered one of you that morning in Lawrence. . . ."

"And Fern Eccles?"

Vance made a weary gesture. "She knew about the bow—that I brought one with me. I talked about it to her a long time ago and forgot she knew. I—had to."

The silence came again. None of them moved. Wayne wondered at this thoughtful, almost solemn silence. After months of terror and tensions, why had they not shouted their accusations?

Vance spoke, voice dead. "I had to—all of you. Not only for me and my brother, but Inez. It was the only way I could . . ."

Frank spoke. "Vengeance is mine, saith the Lord."

"Did the Lord have a wife who lived half the time in another world? Did the Lord try to bring her back to love—and that wasn't enough? And . . ."

Wayne had a momentary, understanding glimpse of a man devil-driven to evil. He was doomed—nothing could stop that but there was another who dwelled in a strange world, as Vance implied. What would be the effect on her of a hang-noose on a public gallows?

A stranger's voice spoke through Wayne. "You've been good in ambush, Vance. You've killed three men. They never harmed you. They made a mistake by joining Quantrell, even though none of them pulled a trigger at Lawrence, or fired a house or took a penny. They pulled out. They tried to forget it. I wasn't even there. But you never asked, did you?"

Vance stared as Wayne continued. "Innocent men, those three, but they're dead now. Joel's innocent, too. You took Fern Eccle's life for nothing. What kind of a man are you!"

Wayne's voice grew sharp and hard. "You came here to kill Hal. Ambush again? A knife? A smile on your face and blood on your hands? Are you as good with a gun face to face as you are in ambush? How good are you, Vance? Make your play. Either that or—hang."

He stepped away from the table. Grayson remained frozen. Lew stood unmoving at the door while the Burruds pressed back, faces deep-grooved and tight. Vance stood motionless, pale face without expression. Only his eyes seemed terribly alive.

Then, slowly, he looked at each of them, reading the truth, seeing the end. He turned to Wayne. His voice held a faint wonder, an acknowledgment of a new fact. "I *would* hang, wouldn't I?"

His hand flashed to his holster, snapping out the gun, thumb dogging back the hammer. Wayne's hand was no real part of him as it streaked to his own gun. He could see only the lift of Vance's weapon toward him. Then his own gun fired with Vance's. His ears rang with thunder, his eyes blinded with the flash of burning powder.

Vance, driven back and around, fell with one out-flung hand touching the closed door by Lew's feet. Blue smoke drifted in lazy coils above the body as the five men looked at one another.

It was late by the time Wayne came home and he rode into the yard dejected by the backwash of tension. He wondered why he felt this strange lassitude rather than triumph. Abbie met him at the door and a single glance told her that Wayne was tired. She poured coffee, placed it on the table near the open window. He thudded into the chair, stared a moment at the checkered cloth and then took a long drink.

He looked up at the open window and his eyes came alive. "We won't have to close the shutters at night—no more."

Abbie grasped the edge of the table. "Wayne! You caught the killer! Who?"

"Ewing Vance. He's dead."

"Vance! No!"

He told her then. She listened, lips parted, breath shallow. He told her how, afterward, the five of them had gone to the mayor. Wayne had persuaded the others to tell the full truth.

"The mayor couldn't believe we had pinned a marshal's star on a killer. He didn't know what to say about all but me being with Quantrell at Lawrence."

"What did he do?"

"Frank told him how they had been sickened at Lawrence and pulled out after the first few minutes. I told him about Joel's two guns—the one at home, the one at the saloon. Vance didn't know there were two when he used the one at the saloon to kill Fern. That's where he slipped and when I found his brother's picture—"

"Then Joel's free?"

"It was the first thing the mayor did. We went to the Gila. We had to tell Inez."

"The poor woman!"

"She went to pieces. But you felt she was not nearly so sorry about Ewing's death as she was that he hadn't killed more of us. She raved and cursed. She said Ewing was a fool. Now he was dead and we were to blame. We'd killed her first husband and now Vance. It sickened us. There was no use trying to explain. She was clean beyond all reason and help. She was still cursing us when we left."

"That scares me, Wayne. She should have been locked up, too."

"There's nothing against her. She killed nobody."

"I guess not." Abbie's face cleared. "But it's all over?"

"Done! There won't be anything said about

Quantrell. People will only know that we caught Vance with evidence of all those killings. He tried to escape and—well, he's dead."

She pulled his head to her breast and his arm circled her waist. She looked out the window. "It's over. That's what counts, darling. We'll not be afraid now."

"It's over . . . hardly seems like it is. You wait for something but when it comes, you can't set your mind to it."

She roughed his hair. "I can, Mr. Nelson! You're tired. I'll fix supper."

They ate by lamplight and the night breeze stirred through the window. Wayne's lassitude passed, to be replaced by a restlessness he couldn't quite understand. He felt as if a great weight was off his shoulders and yet he missed it. He'd be glad when this last vestige of tension was gone. He helped Abbie with the dishes and then prowled about the kitchen, picking up harness bits that needed work, dropping them. Abbie yawned, kissed him and said she was going to bed.

Wayne said, "I can't fix myself for sleep. Be in later."

She kissed him again and went into the bedroom, closing the door against the lamplight. Wayne picked up a harness strap and awl and set himself to the table. The desert silence was soothing and unbroken. He started violently when a light tap sounded on the door. It must be Frank or Jesse, shot through his mind, walking the short distance to talk over the events of the day.

He crossed to the door and flung it open. Inez Vance stood in the lamplight. Her clothing was covered with dust. Her black hair had come loose and damply framed her face. Her violet eyes were dilated and wild. Her lips moved in a smile. "Wayne Nelson, I came to kill you first."

He realized she held a gun leveled on his stomach. He stepped back and she followed him into the room, Colt held steady. He found his voice. "Inez, what foolishness is this?"

"Nothing foolish. First, you killed Edward and today you killed Ewing. That won't end it. Edward told me it wouldn't." She smiled. "He comes back to me, you know. We love one another."

Wayne struck the table, edged around it. She followed. He knew any quick move on his part would cause that hammer, balanced under the delicate thumb, to drop and he'd take the bullet. He could only distract her by talk. He managed to hold his voice to a reasonable tone. "Now, Inez, there's been enough killings. You don't want to go on."

"Edward says I must. He made it clear. There are six of you left. You first, then the two Burruds. I know where to find Grayson and Kearney. Joel will be easy."

Beyond her, Wayne saw the bedroom door

slowly open. He felt a clutch of fear. If Abbie interfered . . . He came slowly up on his toes, ready to spring even as he talked. “But Edward’s dead—”

“I know. You killed him. I saw you. But he comes back.”

Abbie stood framed in the door, eyes wide in horror. Wayne tried to hold Inez’ attention, but some sixth sense warned the woman.

She whirled, gun swinging around as her lips pulled back over beautiful teeth. Wayne lunged, fist knocking the gun muzzle up as it exploded. The bullet thudded into the ceiling as Wayne’s fingers wrapped around her waist and he tried to twist the weapon from her.

She fought, all muscles and steel springs. She nearly writhed free, tried to turn the gun on him. Abbie threw herself on the woman and the three of them went down in a tangle of arms, legs, and skirts. She was as hard to pin down as a fighting snake.

Wayne finally knocked the gun from her hand and Abbie grabbed it. The three of them rolled over again, struck the table. The lamp teetered dangerously, found balance again. Then Abbie had her chance. She brought the muzzle of the gun sharply down on the raven-black head. Inez slumped. Wayne and Abbie clutched the unconscious woman until they realized the fight was over.

Abbie's eyes filled with tears as she dropped the gun and threw herself in Wayne's arms. Her body shook. "She—would have—killed you! She's mad! I've—never been so—scared!"

He gently placed her in a chair. He rolled Inez over, saw that she was not seriously harmed. He snatched a coil of rope from a wall peg and swiftly trussed up the unconscious woman. He snapped orders at Abbie, knowing she needed something to do. "Hitch up the buckboard. We've got to get her to town."

Abbie lifted her tearful face. "Is she—bad hurt?"

"No, knocked out. But she's killing crazy. Probably has been, ever since Lawrence. She has to be locked up. Hurry, now!"

He tied the last knot while Abbie ran out. He paused to look down at the beautiful, placid face. He felt a deep stab of pity and shook his head, awed by the dark future awaiting her. Then his jaw tightened and he checked the knots again.

It was hours before they drove back into the yard, two weary people on the seat of the rattling buckboard. Inez was secure now, safely locked in one of the jail cells. She would never harm anyone again, though she might live, crazed, for years.

Wayne drew rein in the yard. The house looked peaceful and serene in the starlight. He made no effort to climb down, nor did Abbie move. His eyes swung slowly over the house, the yard, his land beyond. Here they would live, and their children. His arm slipped around Abbie's waist.

She turned and kissed him. He looked at the white, soft blur of her face. "Home, Abbie, home for good. No worries now, ever again—for any of us."

"None," she smiled. Suddenly she straightened. "Lew and Lorain! Will they—?"

He laughed. "Them! Make you a bet that right now they're off somewhere under these stars making plans. Their future's good, too. Canby will be mad at first, but he'll get used to a Rebel son-in-law."

Abbie sighed as she leaned against Wayne. "Young lovers! I envy them."

"Hey, now! Are we old?"

He pulled her to him for a long kiss. They broke away, both shaken. Wayne moved to the edge of the seat. "Let's get to the house."

There was a wonderful quiver in her whisper. "Let's!"

Books are produced in the United States using U.S.-based materials

Books are printed using a revolutionary new process called THINKtech™ that lowers energy usage by 70% and increases overall quality

Books are durable and flexible because of Smyth-sewing

Paper is sourced using environmentally responsible foresting methods and the paper is acid-free

Center Point Large Print
600 Brooks Road / PO Box 1
Thorndike, ME 04986-0001 USA

(207) 568-3717

US & Canada:
1 800 929-9108
www.centerpointlargeprint.com